Jessica Gilmore's magical duet

The Life Swap

Embracing a new life...discovering a new love!

Meet Maddison Carter, New York socialite,
and Hope McKenzie, English homebody.
These two women couldn't be more different,
but for six months they will be swapping jobs,
swapping homes and swapping lives!
And in doing so they'll meet two men
who will turn their worlds upside down...

Read Maddison's story in

In the Boss's Castle

and Hope's story in

Unveiling the Bridesmaid

Both available now!

Dear Reader,

Last year I was lucky enough to spend a few days in New York. I was at a conference, and spent far too much time in air-conditioned rooms with no daylight—it was a real shock when I emerged into the hot, sunny, humid city! I did manage to find time to wander into Central Park, visit Bloomingdale's and party at the Waldorf Astoria. I left vowing to return soon—and to set a book there. Luckily my very next book was the second in my The Life Swap duet, and if Maddison, heroine of *In the Boss's Castle*, had left New York for London, then Hope McKenzie, her job swap partner, must be in the Big Apple!

Hope thinks that her six-month stay in New York will be the perfect time to reinvent herself, but three months in she's realising that it takes more than a change of address and a new look to make a real change. When her beloved sister, Faith, asks her to organise a whirlwind wedding and enlist the help of artist Gael O'Connor, Hope finds herself confronting some uncomfortable truths about her past, her life and her heart. Meanwhile Gael has been quite happy with his solitary existence, and the last thing he needs is some buttoned-up English girl turning his world upside down—or so he thinks.

I really loved writing this story—partly because of the wonderfully glamorous setting, but mostly because Gael and Hope were such a delight to discover. I do hope you love them as much as I do.

Jessica x

UNVEILING THE BRIDESMAID

BY
JESSICA GILMORE

First published in Great Britain 2016
By Mills & Boon, an imprint of HarperCollins*Publishers*
1 London Bridge Street, London, SE1 9GF

© 2016 Jessica Gilmore

ISBN: 978-0-263-06528-2

Our policy is to use papers that are natural, renewable and recyclable products and made from wood grown in sustainable forests. The logging and manufacturing processes conform to the legal environmental regulations of the country of origin.

Printed and bound in Great Britain
by CPI Antony Rowe, Chippenham, Wiltshire

A former au pair, bookseller, marketing manager and seafront trader, **Jessica Gilmore** now works for an environmental charity in York, England. Married with one daughter, one fluffy dog and two dog-loathing cats, she spends her time avoiding housework and can usually be found with her nose in a book. Jessica writes emotional romance with a hint of humour, a splash of sunshine and a great deal of delicious food—and equally delicious heroes!

Books by Jessica Gilmore

Mills & Boon Romance

The Life Swap
In the Boss's Castle

Summer Weddings
Expecting the Earl's Baby

The Return of Mrs Jones
Summer with the Millionaire
His Reluctant Cinderella
The Heiress's Secret Baby
A Will, a Wish...a Proposal
Proposal at the Winter Ball

Visit the Author Profile page
at millsandboon.co.uk for more titles.

For Kristy, roommate, cocktail enabler
and partner in crime extraordinaire.

Here's to many more RWA conferences—
and another evening in the rum bar some day. xxx

CHAPTER ONE

Beep, beep, *beeeeeep*.

Hope McKenzie muttered and rolled over, reaching out blindly to mute her alarm, her hand scrabbling to find the 'off' button, the 'pause' button, the *'Please make it stop right now'* button. Only… Hang on a second… She didn't *have* an alarm clock here in New York; she used her phone on the rare occasions when the sun, traffic and humidity didn't wake her first. So what was that noise? And why wouldn't it *stop*?

Beeeeeep.

Whatever it was, it was getting more and more insistent, and louder by the second. Hope pushed herself up, every drowsy limb fighting back as she swung her legs over the metal frame of the narrow daybed and staggered to her feet, glancing at the watch on her wrist. Five-thirty a.m. She blinked, the small room swimming into dim focus, still grey with predawn stillness, the gloom broken only by the glow of the street light, a full floor below her sole window.

Beeeeeep.

It wasn't a fire alarm or a smoke alarm. There were no footsteps pounding down the stairs of the apartment building, no sirens screeching outside, just the high insistent beep coming from the small round table in the window bay. No, coming from her still-open laptop on the small round table in the window bay.

'What the...?' Hope stumbled the few short steps to the table and turned the laptop around to face her. The screen blared into life, bright colour dazzling her still-half-closed eyes, letters jumbling together as she blinked again, rubbing her eyes with one sleepy hand until the words swam into focus.

Faith calling. Accept?

Faith? At this time? Was she in trouble? Hurt? Wait, where was she? Had she left Europe yet? Maybe she'd been framed for drug smuggling? Maybe she had been robbed and lost all her money? Why had Hope left her to travel alone? Why had she swanned off to New York for six months while her baby sister was out there by herself alone and vulnerable? With a trembling hand Hope pressed the enter key to accept the call, pushing her hair out of her eyes, scanning the screen anxiously and pulling up the low neckline of the old, once-white vest top she slept in.

'Faith?' Hope took a deep breath, relief replacing the blind panic of the last few seconds as her sister's tanned, happy face filled the screen. 'Is everything okay?'

'Everything is fab! Oh, did I wake you? Hang on, did I get the time wrong? I thought it would be evening in New York.'

'No, it's morning, we're behind not ahead. But don't worry about that,' she added as her sister's face fell. 'It's lovely to hear from you, to *see* you. Where are you?' Still in Europe somewhere, she thought, doing a quick date calculation. Despite Faith's promises to call and write often, contact with her little sister had been limited since Faith had boarded the Eurostar, just over three months ago, to start her grand tour. She was spending the summer Interrailing around Europe before flying to Australia to begin the global part of her adventures but, unlike her big sister, Faith preferred to go with the flow rather than follow a meticulously thought-out plan. Which meant she could be anywhere.

Hope grinned at her sister, the early hour forgotten. It was okay that Faith had been a little quiet; she was busy exploring and having fun. The last thing she wanted to do was call her fusspot of a big sister who would only nag her about budgets and eating well.

'I'm in Prague.' Faith pulled back from the screen a little to show the room—and view—behind her. She was in some kind of loft, sitting in front of French windows, which led out to a stone balcony. Hope could just make out what must be dazzling views of the river and castle behind. Wow, youth hostels were a lot fancier than she had imagined.

'I thought you arrived in Prague six weeks ago?' Faith hadn't intended spending more than a few days in any one place and Hope was pretty sure her sister had texted her from Prague at the beginning of July.

'I did. I never left. Oh, Hope, it's like a fairy tale here. You would love it.'

'I'm sure I would.' Not that she had been to Prague—or to Paris or to Barcelona or Copenhagen or Rome or any of the other European cities so tantalisingly in reach of London. Their parents had been fans of the great British seaside holiday, rain and all—and since their deaths there had been little money for any kind of holiday. 'But why did you stay in Prague? I thought you wanted to see everything, go everywhere!'

'I did but…well…oh, Hope. I met someone. Someone wonderful and…' Hope peered at the computer screen. Was Faith blushing? Her sister's eyes were soft and her skin glowing in a way that owed nothing to the laptop's HD screen. 'I want you to be happy for me, okay? Because I am. Blissfully. Hope, I'm getting married!'

'Married?' She couldn't be hearing correctly. Her little sister was only nineteen. She hadn't been to university yet, hadn't finished travelling. Heck, she'd barely *started* travelling! More to the point Faith still couldn't handle her own bills, change a fuse or cook anything more complicated than pasta and pesto—and she burnt that two times out of three. How could such a child be getting married? She could only think of one question. 'Who to?'

Her sister didn't answer, turning her head as Hope heard a door bang off-screen. 'Hunter! I got the times wrong. It's still early morning in New York.'

'I know it is, honey. It's not even dawn yet. Did you wake your sister?'

'Oh, she doesn't mind. Come and say hi to her. Hope, this is Hunter, my fiancé.' The pride in Faith's voice, the sweetness in her eyes as she raised them to the tall figure who came to stand next to her, made Hope's throat swell. Her sister had been deprived of a real family at such a young age. No wonder she wanted to strike out and find one of her own. Hope had done her best but she was all too aware what a poor substitute she had been, younger than Faith was now when she took over the reins. Maybe this boy could offer the stability and opportunities she had tried so hard to provide.

And if he couldn't she would be there, making sure he stepped up. She forced a smile, hoping her fierce thoughts weren't showing on her face. 'Hi, Hunter.'

'Hi, it's great to meet you at last. I've heard so much about you.' She summed him up quickly. American. Blond, blue-eyed, clean-cut with an engaging smile. Young. Not quite as young as Faith but barely into his twenties.

'So, how did you two meet?' Hope forced back the words she wanted to say. *Married? You barely know each other! You're just children!* She had promised herself nine years ago she would do whatever it took to make sure Faith was happy—and she had never seen her sister look happier.

'Hunter's an artist.' Pride laced every one of Faith's words. 'He was doing portraits on the Charles Bridge and when I walked past he offered to draw me for free.'

'You had the most beautiful face I'd ever seen,' Hunter said. 'How could I charge you when all I wanted to do was look at you?'

'So I insisted on buying him a drink as a thank you and that was that.' Faith's dark eyes were dreamy, a soft smile playing on her lips. 'Within an hour I knew. We've been inseparable ever since.'

A street artist. Hope's heart sank. However talented he was, that didn't sound too promising as far as setting up a home was concerned and Faith had no career or any idea what she wanted to do after this year was up. She forced another smile. 'How romantic. I can't wait to see the portrait—and meet Hunter in person rather than through a screen.'

'You will! In just over two weeks. That's when we're getting married! In New York and...' Faith adopted a pleading expression Hope knew only too well. 'I was really hoping you'd take care of some of the details for me.'

Hope froze. She knew what 'taking care of some of the details' meant in Faith speak. It meant do everything. And usually she did, happily. Only this was her first time away from her responsibilities in nine years. It was meant to be Hope Getting A Life Time.

Admittedly she hadn't actually got very far yet. Oh, she'd rushed out her first week here in New York and splashed out on a new wardrobe full of bright and striking clothes, had her hair cut and styled. But she couldn't rid herself of feeling like the same old boring Hope. Still, there were three months of her job swap left. She still had every opportunity to do something new and exciting. She just needed to get started.

'Details?' she said cautiously.

'Hunter and I want a small, intimate wedding in New York—just close family and a few friends. His mother will host a big reception party a couple of days later and Hunter says she'll go all out so I think the wedding day should be very simple. Just the ceremony, dinner and maybe some entertainment? You can handle that, can't you? I won't be there until a couple of days before the wedding. Hunter hasn't finished his course and I don't want to leave him alone. Besides, you are so good at organising you'll do a much better job than I ever could. You make everything special.'

Hope's heart softened at the last sentence; she'd

worked so hard to give Faith a perfect childhood. 'Faith, honey, I'm more than happy to help but why so very soon? Why not have it later on and plan it yourself? Travel first, like you arranged.' *Give yourself more time to get to know each other*, she added silently.

'Because we love each other and want to be together as soon as possible. I'm still going travelling—only with Hunter on our honeymoon. Australia and Bali and New Zealand and Thailand. It's going to be the longest and most romantic honeymoon ever. Thank you, Hope, I knew I could rely on you. I'm going to send you some ideas, okay? My measurements for dresses, flowers, colours, you know the kind of thing. But you know my taste. I know whatever you pick will be perfect.'

'Great. That will be really good.' Hope tried to keep her voice enthusiastic but inside she was panicking. How on earth could she work the twelve-hour days her whole office took for granted and plan a wedding in just two weeks? 'Thing is I do have to work, you know, sweetie. My time is limited and I still don't know New York all that well. Are you sure I'm the best person for the job?' She knew the route between her apartment and the office. She knew a nice walk around Central Park. She knew her favourite bookstore and where to buy the perfect coffee. She wasn't sure any of that would be much use in this situation.

Faith didn't seem to notice any of her sister's subtext, ploughing on in breathless excitement. 'There's no budget, Hope, whatever you think is most suitable. Don't worry how much it costs.'

Hope swallowed. 'No budget?' Although she and Faith had never been poor exactly, money had been tight for years. Her parents had been reasonably well insured and the mortgage on their Victorian terrace in north London had been paid off after they died, but after that tax had swallowed up most of their inheritance. She had had to raise Faith on her wages—and at eighteen with little work experience those wages had been pretty meagre. 'Faith, I know that you have your nest egg from Mum and Dad but I don't think it'll stretch to an extravagant wedding.' Was Faith expecting Hope to contribute? She would love to buy her sister her wedding dress, but the words 'no budget' sent chills down her spine.

'Oh, Faith doesn't need to touch her money—I'm taking care of everything,' Hunter said, reappearing behind Faith. 'I've arranged for a credit card to be sent to you.' Hope's eyes flew open at this casual sentence. 'For expenses and deposits and things. Anything you need.'

'For anything I need?' Hope repeated unable to take the words in. 'But…'

'Only the best,' Hunter continued as if she hadn't spoken. 'Anyone gives you any trouble just mention my name—or my mother's, Misty Carlyle. They should fall into line pretty quickly.'

'Mention your name. Okay.' She seemed incapable of doing anything other than parroting his words but the whole situation had just jumped from bizarre to surreal. How did a street artist in Prague have the power to send credit cards for a budget-free wedding shopping spree across the ocean without batting an eyelid? Just who was Faith marrying? A Kennedy?

'Actually, the best person to speak to will be my stepbrother Gael. Gael O'Connor. He only lives a few blocks away from you and he knows everyone. Here,

I'll email you the address and his number and let him know to expect you.' He beamed as if it was all sorted. For Faith and him it was, she supposed. They could carry on being in love in their gorgeous attic room staring out at the medieval castle while Hope battled New York humidity to organise them the perfect wedding.

Well, she would, with the help of Hunter's unexpected largesse. She would make it perfect for her sister if it killed her. Only she wasn't going to do it alone. She was all for equality and there was nothing to say wedding planning had to be the sole preserve of the bride's family after all. As soon as it was a respectable hour she would visit Mr Gael O'Connor and enlist his help. Or press-gang him. She really didn't mind which it was, as long as Faith ended up with the wedding of her dreams.

Gael O'Connor glanced at his watch and tried not to sigh. Sighing hadn't helped last time he checked, nor had pacing, nor had swearing. But when you hired a professional you expected professional behaviour. Not tardiness. Not an entire twenty minutes' worth of tardiness.

He swivelled round to stare out of the floor-to-ceiling windows that lined one whole side of his studio. Usually looking out over Manhattan soothed him or inspired him, whatever he needed. Reminded him that he had earned this view, this space. Reminded him that he mattered. But today all it told him was that he was taking a huge gamble with his career and his reputation.

Twenty-five minutes late. He had to keep busy, not waste another second. Turning, he assessed once again the way the summer morning light fell on the red velvet chaise longue so carefully positioned in the middle of the room, the only piece of furniture in the large studio. His bed and clothes were up on the mezzanine, the kitchen and bathroom were tucked away behind a discreet door at the end of the apartment. He liked to keep this main space clutter-free. He needed to be able to concentrate.

Only right now there was nothing to concentrate on except the seconds ticking away.

Gael resumed pacing. Five minutes, he would give her five more minutes and if she hadn't arrived by then he would make sure she never worked in this city again. Hang on. Was that the buzzer? It had never been more welcome. He crossed the room swiftly. 'Yes?'

'There's a young lady to see you, sir. Name of…'

'Send her up.' At last. Gael walked back over to the windows and breathed in the view: the skyscrapers dominating the iconic skyline, the new, glittering towers shooting up around him as New York indulged in a frenzied orgy of building, the reassuring permanence of the old, traditional Upper East Side blocks maintaining their dignified stance on the other side of his tree-lined street. He shifted from foot to foot. He needed to use this restless energy while it coursed through him—not waste it in frustration.

The creak of the elevator alerted him to his visitor's imminent arrival. No lobby, not when you had the penthouse; the elevator opened right into the studio.

And he did have the penthouse. Not as a gift, not as a family heirloom but because he had worked for it and bought it. Not one of his friends would ever understand the freedom that gave him.

The doors opened with an audible swish and heels

tapped tentatively onto the wooden floor. 'Er...hello?' English. He hadn't expected that. Not that he cared what she sounded like; he wasn't interested in having a conversation with her.

'You're late.' Gael didn't bother turning round. Usually he made time to greet the women, put them at their ease before they got started but he was too impatient for the niceties today. 'There's a robe on the chaise. You can change in the bathroom.'

'Excuse me?'

'The bathroom.' He nodded to the end of the room. 'There's a hanger for your clothes. Go and strip. You can keep the robe on until I've positioned you properly if you prefer.' Some did, others were quite happy to wander nude from the bathroom across the floor to the chaise. He didn't mind either way.

'My clothes? You want me to take them off?'

'Well, yes. That's why you're here, isn't it?'

He moved around to face her at the exact same moment she let out a scandalised-sounding, 'No! Of course not. Why would you think that?'

Who on earth was this? Dark-haired, dark-eyed, petite with a look of outraged horror. She was pretty enough, beautiful even—if you liked the 'big dark eyes in a pale face' look. But he was expecting an Amazonian redhead with a knowing smile and whatever and whoever this girl was she certainly wasn't that.

'Because I was expecting someone who was supposed to be doing exactly that,' Gael said drily. 'But you are not what I ordered. Too short for a start, although you do have an interesting mouth.'

'Ordered?' Her cheeks reddened as the outrage visibly ratcheted up several notches. 'I'm sorry that I'm not your takeout from Call Girls Are Us but I think you should check before you start asking complete strangers to strip.'

'I'm not the one who has gatecrashed their way past the doorman. Who are you? Did Sonia send you?'

'Sonia? I don't know any Sonia. There's clearly been some kind of mix-up. You *are* Gael O'Connor, aren't you?' She sounded doubtful, taking a cautious step back as if he might pounce any second.

He ignored her question. 'If you don't know Sonia then why are you here?'

She took a deep breath. 'My sister is getting married and...'

'Great. Congratulations. Look, I don't do weddings. I don't care how much you offer. Now, I'm more than a little busy so if you'll excuse me I have to make a call. I'm sure you can find your own way out. You seemed to have no trouble finding your way in.'

The dark-haired woman stared at him, incredulity all over her face as he pulled his phone out of his pocket. Ignoring his unwanted visitor, Gael scrolled through what felt like an endless stream of emails, notifications and alerts. His mouth compressed. Nothing from the agency. With a huff of impatience he found their name and pressed call. They had better have a good explanation. The phone rang once, twice—he tapped his foot with impatient rhythm—three times before a voice sang out, 'Unique Models, how may I help?'

'Gael O'Connor here. It's now...' He glanced up at the digital clock on the otherwise stark grey walls. 'It's nine a.m. and the model I booked for eight-thirty has yet to show up.'

'Gael, lovely to speak to you. I am so sorry, I meant to call you before but I literally haven't had time. It's been crazy, you wouldn't believe.'

'Try me.'

'Sonia was booked yesterday for a huge ad campaign—only it was a last-minute replacement so she had to literally pack and fly. I saw her onto the plane myself last night. International perfume ad, what an opportunity. Especially for a model who is...' the booker's voice lowered conspiratorially '...outsize. So we are going to have to reschedule your booking I am so sorry. Or could I send someone else? We have some lovely redheads if that's what you require or was it the curvier figure you were looking for?'

With some difficulty Gael managed not to swear. Send someone else? An image of the missing Sonia flashed through his mind: the knowing expression in her green catlike eyes, the perfect amount of confident come-hitherness he needed for the centrepiece of his first solo exhibition. 'No. I can't simply replace her, nor can I rebook. I've put the time aside right now.'

After all, the exhibition *was* in just five weeks.

'Sonia will be back in just a couple of days. All I can do is apologise for the delay but...'

It would help, he thought bitterly, if the booker sounded even remotely sorry. She would be—he would never use a Unique model again. He hung up on her bored pretence for an apology. Once Sonia was back she would be of no use to him. Unlike his photographs Gael didn't want the subjects of his paintings to be known faces. Their anonymity was part of the point. He spent too much time documenting the bright and the beautiful. For this he wanted real and unknown.

His hand curled into a fist as he faced the bitter facts. He still had to paint the most important piece for his very first exhibition and he had no model lined up. He mentally ran through his contacts but no one obvious came to mind. Most of the models he knew were angular, perfect for photography, utterly useless for this.

Damn.

'Mr O'Connor.'

Palming his phone, Gael directed a frustrated glance over at his unwanted intruder. 'I thought you'd left,' he said curtly. She was standing stiffly by the elevator, leaning towards it as if she longed to flee—although nobody was stopping her, quite the contrary. Gael allowed his gaze to travel down her, assessing her suitability. Before he had only looked at what she lacked compared to the model he was expecting to see; she was much shorter, slight without the dramatic curves, ice to Sonia's fire. She wore her bright clothing like a costume, her dark hair waving neatly around her shoulders like a cloak. Her eyes were huge and dark but the wariness in them seemed engrained.

She took another step back. 'Do you mind?'

'It is my studio...' he drawled. That was better; indignation brought some more colour into her cheeks, red into her lips.

'I am not some painting that you can just look at in that way. As if...as if...' She faltered.

But he knew exactly what she had been going to say and finished off her sentence. 'As if you were naked.'

He had lit the fuse and she didn't disappoint; her eyes filled with fire, her cheeks now dusky pink. She would make a very different centrepiece from the one he had envisioned but he could work with those eyes, with that innocent sensuality, with the curve of her full mouth.

He nodded at her. 'Come over here. I want to show you something.'

Gael didn't wait to see if she would follow; he knew that she would. He strode to the end of the studio and turned over the four unframed canvases leaning against the brick wall. There would be twenty pictures in total. Ten had been framed and were stored at the gallery, another five were with the framers. These four, the most recent, were waiting their turn.

He heard a sharp intake of breath from close behind him. He took a step back to stand beside her and looked at the paintings, trying to look at them with fresh eyes, to see what she saw even though he knew each and every brush stroke intimately.

'Why are all the women lying in the same position?'

Gael glanced over at the red chaise standing alone in the middle of the studio, knowing her eyes had followed his, that she too could see each of the women lying supine, their hair pulled back, clad only in jewellery, their faces challenging, confident, aware and revelling in their own sensual power.

'Do you know *Olympia*?'

Her forehead creased. 'Home of the Greek gods?'

'No, it's a painting by Manet.'

She shook her head. 'I don't think so.'

'It was reviled at the time. The model posed naked, in the same position as each of these,' he waved a hand at his canvases, at the acres of flesh: pink, cream, coffee, ebony. 'What shocked nineteenth-century France wasn't her nudity, it was her sexuality. She wasn't some kind of goddess, she was portraying a prostitute. Nudes at that time were soft, allegorical, not real sensual beings. *Olympia* changed all that. I have one more painting to produce before my exhibition begins in just over a month.' His mouth twisted at the thought. 'But as you must have heard my model has gone AWOL and I can't afford to lose any more time. I want you to pose for me. Will you?'

Her eyes were huge, luminous with surprise and, he noticed uncomfortably, a lurking fear. 'Me? You want *me* to pose? For you? On that couch? Without my clothes? Absolutely not!'

CHAPTER TWO

HE WANTED HER to *what*? Hope stepped back and then again, eyeing Gael O'Connor nervously. But he lost interest the second she uttered her emphatic refusal, turning away from her with no attempt to persuade her. Hope could see her very presence fading from his mind as he began to scroll through his phone again, muttering names speculatively as he did so.

Maybe she should just go, try and arrange this wedding by herself. She looked around, eyes narrowing as she took on the vast if largely empty room, the huge windows, the high ceiling, the view… This much space, on the Upper East Side? Hope did some rapid calculations and came up with seven figures. At the very least. Her own studio would fit comfortably in one corner of the room and the occupant probably wouldn't even notice she was there. Hunter had said that his stepbrother could get her into all the right places and this address, this room, Gael's utter certainty that he commanded the world indicated that her brother-in-law-to-be hadn't been lying.

Hope cleared her throat but her voice still squeaked with nerves. 'Hi, I think we got off on the wrong foot. I'm Hope McKenzie and I'm here because your brother—stepbrother—is engaged to my sister.'

He didn't look up from his phone. 'Which one?'

'Which what?'

'Stepbrother. I have...' he paused, the blue eyes screwed up in thought '...five. Although two of those are technically half-brothers, I suppose, and too young to be engaged anyway.'

'Hunter. Hunter Carlyle. He met my sister, Faith, in Prague and...'

'Hunter isn't my stepbrother. He *was*,' Gael clarified. 'But his mother divorced my father a decade ago, which makes him nothing at all to me.'

'But he said...'

'He would, he clings to the idea of family. He's like his mother that way. It's almost sweet.'

Hope took a deep breath, feeling like Alice wrestling with Wonderland logic. 'As I said, he's engaged to my sister and I was wondering...'

'I wouldn't worry. I know he's young. How old is your sister?'

Was she ever going to say what she had come here to say? It had been a long time since she had felt so wrong-footed at every turn—although being asked to strip by a strange man at nine a.m. would wrong-foot anyone. 'Nineteen, but...'

He nodded. 'Starter marriages rarely last. There will be a prenup, of course, but don't worry, the Carlyles are very generous to their exes. Just ask my dad.' Bitterness ran through his voice like a swirl of the darkest chocolate.

'Starter marriages?' This was getting worse. Was

she going to be able to formulate a whole sentence any time soon?

He raised an eyebrow. 'That's why you're here, isn't it? To ask me to stop the wedding? I wouldn't worry. Hunter's a good kid and, like I said, the prenups are generous. Your sister will come out of this a wealthy woman.'

Hope's lips compressed. 'My sister is marrying Hunter because she loves him.' She pushed the part of her brain whispering that Faith had only known Hunter for six weeks ruthlessly aside. 'And I am sure he loves her.' Based on a two-minute conversation through a computer screen but she wasn't going to give Gael O'Connor the satisfaction of seeing her voice any doubts. 'They want to get married, here in New York, two weeks on Thursday and they asked me to organise the wedding.'

Gael's mouth pursed into a soundless whistle. 'I wonder what Misty will say to that. She prides herself on her hostessing skills.'

'I believe she is holding a party on Long Island shortly after. A small and intimate wedding, that's what Faith's asked for and that's what I am going to give her. But it's going to be the best small and intimate wedding any bride ever had. Hunter thought you would be able to help me but it's very clear that you are far too busy to get involved in anything as trivial as a starter marriage. I won't bother you any more. Good day.'

Head up, shoulders straight and she was going to walk right out of here. So she might not have Gael O'Connor's connections; she had a good head on her shoulders and determination. That should do it.

'Hope, wait.' There was a teasing note in his voice

that sent warning shivers through her. Hope was pretty
sure that whatever he wanted she wasn't going to like it.

'Pose for me and I'll help you give your sister the
perfect wedding. I can, you know,' he added as she
gaped at him. 'My little black book...' he held up his
phone '...is filled with everyone and anyone you need
from designers to restaurateurs. You do this and your
sister will have the wedding of her dreams. And that's
a promise.' His gaze swept over her assessingly, that
same lazy exploration that made her feel stripped to
the skin. She shivered, her heart thumping madly as
each nerve responded to his insolence.

Mad, bad, definitely dangerous to know. She was
horribly out of her depth. 'I...look, this isn't something
you can just throw at someone. It's a big deal.'

A small smile curved his mouth. It didn't reach his
eyes; she had a sense it seldom did. 'Hope, life modelling is a perfectly respectable thing to do. Men and
women of all ages and body shapes do it day in, day
out.'

She cast a quick glance at the canvases still facing
out, at the exposed flesh and the satisfied, confident
gazes. 'But these aren't men and women of all ages and
shapes,' she pointed out. 'They are all women and they
are all beautiful, all sexy.'

'That's because of the theme of the show. If Olympia had been a middle-aged man then we wouldn't be
having this conversation. It'll be quite intensive. I'll
need a week or so of your time, first a few sketches
and then the actual painting. The first session is the
most important—I need to know that you're comfortable with the pose, with the jewellery you choose and
its symbolism. The tricky bit is finding the right mood.

The other models have spent some time thinking about their past, about their sexuality and what it means to them; the original Olympia saw sex as business and that comes across in her portrait. She is in control of her body, what it offers.'

Which meant, she supposed, that he thought she could portray sexuality. Awareness quivered through her at the idea. Awareness of his height, of the lines of his mouth, the steeliness in his eyes. It was an attractive combination, the dark hair, such a dark chocolate it was almost black, and warm olive skin with the blue-grey eyes.

Eyes fastened solely on her. Hope swallowed. It had been a long time since anyone had intimated that they found her sexy. Attractive, useful, nice. But not sexy. It was a seductive idea. Hope stared at the red couch and tried to imagine it: her hair piled up, pulling at the nape of her neck, the coolness of a pendant heavy on her naked breast, the way the rubbed velvet would feel against the tender skin on her thighs and buttocks, against her back.

How it would feel to have that steely gaze directed intently on her, to have him focus on every hair, every dimple, every curve—Hope sucked in her stomach almost without realising it—every scar.

Hope's cheeks flamed. How could she even be having this conversation? She didn't wear a bikini, for goodness' sake, let alone nothing at all. If she could shower in her clothes she would. As for tapping into her sexuality…she swallowed painfully. How could you tap into something that didn't actually exist? Even if she had the time and the inclination to lie there exposed she didn't have the tools.

'You're talking to the wrong woman.' Her voice was cold and clipped, her arms crossed as if she could shield herself from his speculative sight. 'Even if I wanted to model for you—which I don't—I don't have the time. I have a job to do, a job which takes up twelve hours of every day and often my weekend as well. I have no idea how I am going to sort out a wedding in less than three weeks and still keep Brenda Masterson happy but, well, that's my problem. I will manage somehow. I don't need or want your help. Goodbye, Mr O'Connor. As you don't consider Hunter to be part of your family I doubt we'll meet again.'

Hope swivelled and turned, heading for the door, glad of the heels, glad of the well-cut, summery clothes and the extra confidence they gave her. She was new Hope now, new Hope in New York City. She had time to invest in her career, a little money to invest in herself and the way she looked. Any day now she would try her hand at salsa or Zumba or running, join a book club and go to interesting lectures. So she had missed out on being a young adult? It wasn't too late to become the person she once dreamed of being.

But first she would organise her sister's wedding. And not by taking off her clothes and posing for some artist no matter how much she liked the way his eyes dwelled on her. Eyes she could feel follow her as she crossed the room, and pushed the button to summon the lift. Eyes that seemed to strip her bare and see straight through the thin veneer of confidence she had plastered on.

If he did paint her she knew it wouldn't just be her body that would be bared for the world to see. It would be her soul as well. And that was a risk she would never be able to take.

'Did you say you work for Brenda Masterson?'

She paused. One minute he was dismissing her, the next making her an outrageous proposal—and now small talk? She turned and glared at him, hoping he took her impatient message on board. 'Yes, I work at DL Media. I'm in New York on a job swap as Brenda's assistant.' Brenda's very late assistant. She was probably focussing that famously icy glare right at Hope's vacant desk right this moment.

Gael kept her gaze as he pressed his phone to his ear, a mocking smile playing on his well-cut lips. 'Brenda? Is that you?'

What? He knew Brenda? He had said he knew everybody but she didn't think he meant her boss.

'Hi. It's Gael. Yes, I'm good, how about you? I've been having a think about that retrospective. Uh-huh. It's a good offer you made me but there's some work I need to do first, going through the old blogs, through the old photos.' He paused as Brenda spoke at some length, her words indiscernible to Hope.

She shifted from foot to foot, wishing she had worn less strappy heels in this heat—and that she had catlike hearing. This job was her chance to be noticed, to stop being Kit Buchanan's loyal and mousy assistant and to be someone with prospects and a real career—if Gael O'Connor messed this up for her she would knock him out with one of his own paintings...

'As it happens,' Gael continued smoothly, 'I have your assistant here. Yes, very cute. Love the accent.' He winked at Hope and she clenched her jaw. 'It would be great if you could spare her for a couple of weeks to help me with the archiving and labelling, maybe start to put together some copy. Yeah. Absolutely. You're a doll, Brenda. Thanks.'

A what? Hope was pretty sure nobody had ever called Brenda Masterson a doll before and lived through the experience. Gael clicked his phone off and smiled over at Hope. 'Good news. You're mine for the next couple of weeks.'

She *what*? In his dreams. And she was going to tell him so just as soon as she had the perfect withering put-down—and when she had answered the call vibrating insistently through her phone. Hope pulled the phone out of her pocket and the words hovering on her lips dried up when she saw Brenda's name flashing on the screen. She didn't need to take a course in fortune telling to predict what this call would be about. With a withering look in Gael's direction, which promised that this conversation was totally not over, Hope answered the call, tension twisting in her stomach.

'Brenda, hi. Sorry, I'm on my way in.' Damn, why had she apologised? She hadn't realised just how much she said 'sorry' or 'excuse me' until she moved to New York where no one else seemed to spend their time apologising for occupying space or wanting to get by or just existing. Every time she said sorry to Brenda she felt her stock fall a little further.

'Absolutely not. Stay right where you are. I didn't realise you knew Gael O'Connor.' Was that admiration in Brenda's voice? Great, three months into her time here and she had finally made her boss sit up and take notice—not through her hard work, initiative or talent but because of some guy she'd only met this morning.

'My sister is engaged to his stepbrother. Ex-stepbrother.'

She couldn't have this conversation in front of him, not as he leaned against the wall, arms folded and an annoying *Gotcha* smirk on his admittedly handsome face. Hope walked past him, heading for the door she'd seen at the other end of the apartment. It might lead to his red room of pain or whatever but she'd take the risk. Actually it led to a rather nice kitchen—an oddity in a city where nobody seemed to have space to cook. It was a little overdone on the stainless-steel front for Hope's tastes and ranked highly on the 'terrifying appliances I don't know how to use and can't even guess what they're for' scale but it was still rather impressive. And very clean. Maybe having a kitchen was a status thing, the using of it optional.

She shut the door firmly behind her. 'I don't know Gael O'Connor exactly. I only met him today to discuss wedding plans.'

'You've obviously impressed him. Let's keep it that way. I'm seconding you to work with him over the next two weeks. I want regular updates and I want him kept sweet. If you can do that then I can promise that all the right people will know how helpful you've been, Hope. It wouldn't surprise me if you got your pick of roles at the end of this secondment here or back in London. After all, as you've probably heard by now, Kit Buchanan's resigned from the London office inconveniently taking my assistant with him. Maybe we could arrange for you to stay here, if you wanted to, that is…'

Hope's breath caught in her throat. *Keep him sweet?* Did Brenda know just what he wanted her to do? Was she suggesting that nude modelling was part of her job description? Because Hope was pretty sure she'd missed that clause unless it fell somewhere under 'any other business.'

But Brenda had also tapped into a worry that Hope had been trying very hard not to think about. Her role in London had been working as a PA for the undoubtedly brilliant if often frustrating Kit Buchanan. Yet in less than three months he had fallen in love with Maddison Carter, her job-swap partner and owner of the tiny if convenient Upper East Side studio Hope was currently living in. And that had changed everything. She hadn't expected to feel so *lost* when she'd heard the news, almost grief stricken. It wasn't that she was jealous exactly. She wasn't in love with Kit. She didn't really have a crush on him either, although he had a nice Scottish accent, was handsome in an 'absent-minded professor' kind of way and, crucially, was the only single man under thirty she spent any time with. But Kit's resignation meant that in three months she would be returning to a new manager—and possibly a different, less fulfilling role.

It was a long time since Hope had dreamed of archaeology; she'd pushed those dreams and any thought of university aside after her parents died, starting instead as an office junior at a firm of solicitors close to her Stoke Newington home. But when she had moved to DL Media three years ago Kit had been quick to see potential in his PA and ensured there had been a certain amount of editorial training and events work in her duties. There was no guarantee a new manager would feel the same way. But if Brenda was impressed with her then who knew what opportunities would open up? Hope took a deep breath and tried to clear her head.

'Why does Gael need an assistant from DL Media?' *And why me?* she silently added.

'Because Gael O'Connor is planning a retrospective of his photographs and the blog that catapulted him into the public eye and I want to make sure that he chooses DL Media as his partner when he does so. I've been courting him and his agent for nearly a year and got nowhere. They say that his archive is incredible, that he could bring down careers, end marriages with his photos,' Brenda's voice was full of longing. 'I can smell the sales now. This could be huge, Hope, and you could be part of it straight from the start. I want you to get me those photos and the anecdotes that accompany them. Help him sort out his archive and make sure that at the end he is so impressed he signs on the dotted line of the very generous contract we offered him. Take as long as you need, do whatever you have to do but get that signature for me. You have an in. He asked for you, your sister is marrying someone he's close to. Anyone would kill for that kind of connection. Exploit it. If you do then I guarantee you a nice promotion and a secure future here at DL Media...'

Hope didn't need to ask what would happen if she failed—or if she refused. Back to England in ignominy and coffee-making, minute-taking and contract-typing-up for the rest of her days. If she was lucky. But if she agreed then she was not only getting a huge boost up the career ladder but she would also be away from the office, out from under Brenda's eye and could grab the time to sort out Faith's wedding. Damn Gael O'Connor, he had her exactly where he wanted her.

'Okay,' she said, injecting as much confidence into

her voice as she could manage. 'I'll do it. You don't have to worry, Brenda. I won't let you down.'

Gael couldn't hear Hope's conversation with her boss but he didn't need to. Hope was as good as his. He'd met Brenda Masterson several times and he knew her type; her eyes were fixed firmly on the prize and she wasn't going to let anything or anyone get in her way.

The kitchen door opened and Hope stalked through, her colour high but her eyes bright with determination. 'I suppose you think you are very clever,' she said. 'Of course some might call it blackmail…'

'Call what blackmail? Your boss wants my archive and I need help organising it. Seems like a fair trade to me.' But Gael couldn't stop the smile playing around his lips. 'You should thank me. I'm much less of a clock watcher than Brenda. You might even get some wedding organising done while you're here. In fact you can have today to get started. Consider it my wedding gift to the happy couple.'

'Is there even an archive or is this just some kind of ruse to keep me here?'

Gael stilled. He was so used to people knowing who he was, what he was, that the scorn in her all too candid eyes took him back. Back to the days before *Expose*. The days when he was nothing. 'I see. You think this is a ploy to get you to pose? Get real, princess. I may have asked you to sit for me but I don't beg and I certainly don't coerce. Every one of those women over there…' He nodded over at the canvases. 'They came to me freely.'

Her forehead creased. 'So why did you ask Brenda if I could work for you?'

'Because I was planning on saying yes to Brenda's offer anyway and this saves me the hassle of finding an assistant. Because I won't mind how you organise your time as long as the archiving work gets done so this way you can pop out to look at venues or cakes or whatever else you need to do. Not to force you into anything. Nobody is keeping you here against your will, Rapunzel, there's no escape ladder needed. You can leave at any time.'

Hope looked over at the chaise, a frown still creasing her forehead. 'I'm sorry, I just thought…you said you wouldn't help me with the wedding and then this all happened so fast.'

'I'm *not* helping you. I'm giving you time but that's all you'll get out of me. I have a model to find and paint, an exhibition to put on and an archive to explain to you and oversee. The wedding's your problem, not mine. Unless you change your mind about the picture, in which case I'll keep my end of the bargain and help you but, like I said, your decision. It's not part of your duties here. I have no interest in a reluctant subject.'

She took a visible deep breath, her eyes clouded, her forehead still wrinkled with thought. She was close to a decision but whether that decision was changing her mind and posing or walking out and telling him to go to hell he had no idea.

It was intriguing, this unpredictability.

'If I said yes…' She stopped, her eyes wary again.

He should be feeling triumphant. He almost had her, he could tell. But Hope McKenzie wasn't like his usual subjects. They were all eager for him to tell their stories with his paintbrush—she was all secrets and disguises. 'Before we go any further, I need you to know exactly what you're getting into.'

'I lie there and you paint me. Right?' The words were belligerent but her eyes dark with fear.

'It's not easy being a life model. It's a skill. You have to keep the same pose for hours. No complaining about being cold, or achy or hungry.'

'Okay.'

'I asked each model to wear some jewellery that meant something to them. Something very personal.' He pointed over at one canvas. 'That girl there, Anna? She's wearing pins in her hair she wore on her wedding day. This lady, Ameena, she's wearing gold necklaces and bangles gifted to her by her parents when she emigrated to the US.'

'And they have to be naked. I mean, I would have to be. Totally. I couldn't, instead of jewellery have a scarf or something. It's just…'

'Sorry.' And he was. It wasn't easy for even the most seasoned model to lie there so exposed to him and even though his other models had been enthusiastic about the project they had still found posing difficult, embarrassment covered in a multitude of ways, by jokes, by attempted seduction, by detachment.

'That's okay.'

It didn't seem okay; her hands were twisting together in an attempt to hide a slight shake.

'The last thing is probably the most important. If you model then I need you to think about sex. What it means to you, good and bad. I need you to think about that the whole time I paint you. I know that's an odd request but it's the theme of the paintings and it needs to show in your eyes, on your face. If it helps I can play any music you want, audiobooks, relaxation tapes—whatever makes you comfortable.'

It was odd, he'd had this conversation many times before and he had never felt so like some kind of libertine before. Every other model had known exactly why she was there, had volunteered for this. It was business, not personal.

But this time it felt horribly personal and he had no idea why.

'Think about sex?'

'Is that a problem?'

'It might be.' Her colour was even higher, rivalling the red of the chaise. 'You see, I haven't actually... I don't... I'm not...what I'm trying to say is...' she swallowed '... I'm a virgin. So I don't think I can lie there and think about something I know nothing about. Do you?'

CHAPTER THREE

'THANK YOU. No, I see. Yes. Absolutely. Thank you.'
Hope clicked her phone off and resisted the urge to
throw it off the fire escape and let it smash into smith-
ereens. Another hotel she could cross off her 'possibles'
list. Three hours of calling and emailing and she still
hadn't made one appointment.

She scanned the list she'd made the second she'd arrived home. It had all seemed so simple then.

1. Find a dress
2. Sort out flowers
3. Ceremony—where????
4. Read through Brenda's six zillion emails
*5. Try and show Gael O'Connor that you're com-
petent and professional and not a complete bas-
ket case...*

Hope resisted the urge to bang her head on the
wrought-iron railing she was propped up against. She
might have managed to steal one day of wedding planning from Gael O'Connor's manipulative hands but
where had it got her? Every venue she had phoned had
either laughed at her incredulously or sounded vaguely

scandalised. 'A wedding? In two weeks? Ma'am, this isn't Vegas. I suggest you try City Hall.' And as for a dress...you would think she had asked them to spin straw into gold, not supply one white dress, US size four.

And yes, she could try City Hall. And she could pop into any one of a dozen shops and pull a dress off the racks and it would do. And she could book a table in a five-star restaurant and the food would be great. But it wouldn't be special. It wouldn't show Faith just how much Hope loved her. It wouldn't make up for the fact that Faith would have no proud father walking her down the aisle, no mother in a preposterous hat wiping away tears and beaming proudly. Faith deserved the best and Hope had vowed nine years ago that she would have it. This wedding wasn't going to beat her, no, not if it killed her. Her baby sister would have the finest and most romantic whirlwind wedding New York had ever seen. She just needed to work out how and where.

Hope took a sip of coffee and stared at her laptop, balancing precariously on her open window ledge, hoping it would give her some much-needed inspiration. Maybe if she had spent a little more time actually in the city itself and less time either in the office or here, sunning herself on the fire escape outside her apartment window, she might actually have some unique and doable ideas. Okay. She was in the greatest city in the world, how could her mind be so blank? 'New York,' she muttered. 'New York.'

A ping from her laptop broke her half-hearted reverie and Hope looked across at it, sighing when she saw yet another email from Brenda flashing on her screen. What was going on? She had never seen her famously ice-cool boss this het up over anyone. Hunter had said that Gael knew everybody and what was it Brenda had whispered? He had the power to finish careers and destroy marriages? Remembering the mocking smile and the coldness in the blue-grey eyes, Hope didn't doubt it.

Setting her coffee cup to one side, she scrambled onto her knees and pulled up her internet browser. 'Who exactly are you, Gael O'Connor?' With a guilty look around, as if the starling on the rail above could see her snooping, Hope pressed Enter and waited. She wasn't sure what to expect but it wasn't the lines and lines of links that immediately filled her screen. Headlines, photos, articles—and a comprehensive Wikipedia entry.

Gael O'Connor. Photographer. Blogger. Society darling. It looked as if he didn't just *know* the New York scene—he dictated it, moving through it, camera at the ready, creating instant stars.

Nowhere would say no to him. Nowhere would tell him that two weeks was impossible. No one would suggest that Gael O'Connor tried City Hall...

Damn.

Her choice was stark. Either she compromised on the wedding or she agreed to Gael's demands and posed for him. If he still wanted her, that was, after her moment of hysterical oversharing. Hope groaned, slumping back again against the sun-hot railing. It was going to be bad enough facing him the next day in a working capacity, how on earth could she bring up the whole naked posing thing? Maybe she should run away instead. Somewhere no one would ever find her—she'd bet Alaska was nice and anonymous and a nice bracing contrast to this never-ending humidity.

At that moment her phone rang. She didn't recognise the number and answered it cautiously. After this morning's 'blurting out secret personal information to a stranger' debacle she'd probably tell the telemarketer about the time she wet herself in playgroup or when she shoplifted a chocolate bar when she was five—and how her mother made her take it back with a note of apology. 'Hope speaking.'

'How's the wedding planning coming along?' A gravelly voice, like the darkest chocolate mixed with espresso.

Hope glared at her laptop. How had Gael known she was thinking of contacting him? Maybe he had sold his soul to the devil and just thinking about him summoned him? 'Great!' Just a little lie.

'That's good. I was worried that two weeks' notice might be too tight for any of the really good venues.'

'How sweet of you to worry but actually I have it all under control.' Another little lie. Any moment her nose was going to start growing.

'Excellent. So you'll be here nice and early tomorrow to start work?'

'I can't wait.' Yes, she'd better hope that long noses were going to be fashionable this year because the way she was going hers was going to be longer than her outstretched arm.

'All you need is your laptop and a lot of patience. I do hope you like cataloguing.'

'I love it. I'd hate to get in your way though, while you're painting. I could work from the office or from mine if that's more convenient.' *Please let it be more convenient.*

'There's nothing to get in the way of. I haven't found

a model yet.' The mockery slipped from Gael's voice, his frustration clear.

'Oh.'

It was a sign. A big neon sign. He still needed a model and she, like it or not, needed his help. Hope took a deep breath. 'Look, Gael. I hate to deprive you of the joy of wedding planning and it looks like we're going to be spending some time together anyway so...' It was even harder to say the words than she'd anticipated.

'So?'

He knew, she could tell, but was no doubt taking some unholy satisfaction from making her spell it out.

'So I can pose. For your picture. If you still want me after, well, if you still want me...' She wasn't going to own up to her virgin status again. She still couldn't believe she had mentioned it at all, said it out loud. To a complete stranger. A state of affairs she had barely acknowledged over the last few years, pushing the thought away as soon as it occurred. Her own secret shame. Hope McKenzie, old before her time, withered, sexless.

'An intriguing offer.'

She tried not to grind her teeth. 'Not really,' she said as breezily as she could. 'I didn't exactly give you an answer, if you remember.' No, she had backed away, muttered something about needing to get things sorted, said, 'Thank you for the offer to take today to start planning and see you tomorrow, thank you very much...' and scarpered as fast as her feet could carry her, out of the studio and back to the safety of her own apartment.

'I thought your mad dash out of the studio was answer enough. Why the sudden change of heart?'

Hope never admitted to needing anyone; she didn't intend to start now. 'You need someone to start straight away and spend the next two weeks at your beck and call. Well, whether I like it or not I am already at your beck and call. It makes sense.'

'How very giving of you. So you're offering because it's convenient?'

Her fingers curled into a fist. *He'd asked her*—why on earth was she the one working to convince him? 'And although I am more than capable of sorting this wedding alone it would be foolish of me not to use all the resources available. I barely know the city but you live here, your input could save me a lot of wasted effort—and this is the only way you'll help. I'm big enough to admit that if I want Faith to have the best wedding possible then I need to involve you.'

'Another altruistic motive.' Hope's cheeks heated at the sardonic note in Gael's voice. 'And very laudable but you've seen the other portraits. Sacrificial victim isn't the look I'm going for. It's not enough for you to agree to pose. I need you to want it. Tell me, Hope. Do you want it?' His voice had lowered to a decadent pitch, intimately dark. Hope swallowed.

Did she want to pose for him? Lie on that chaise, his eyes on every exposed inch of skin?

Hope stared out through the black iron railings. She knew the view by heart. The buildings opposite, the tops of the trees. This was where she hung out with a coffee and a book or her laptop, too scared to venture out of the comfort zone she'd carved for herself. She didn't mean to speak but somehow the words came spilling out. Another sad confession. 'I meant to shake things up when I moved here. New York was my chance to reinvent myself. I started, I bought new clothes and chopped off some of my hair and thought that would be enough. But I'm still the same. I don't know how to talk to people any more, not when it doesn't involve work or superficial stuff. I don't...' She hesitated. 'I don't know how to make friends, how to have fun. Maybe this will help me loosen up. It'll be a talking point if nothing else.'

'You want me to help you loosen up?' Her pulse quickened at the velvet in his voice.

'Yes. No! Not you exactly. What I mean is that I need to try something different, to be different. Posing for you will be new, unexpected.'

'Okay. Let's try this.'

She hadn't known how tightly she was wound waiting for his answer, how the world had fallen away until it was just the two of them, sharing an intimate space even though they were half a mile apart, until he agreed.

'Great.' She inhaled a shaky breath. 'So what now? Do you want me to come over and...?' Her voice trailed off. How was she going to do it if she couldn't even say it?

The laughter in his voice confirmed he was probably thinking the same thing. 'Not today. I think we need to warm up a little first. You, Hope McKenzie, have just admitted you need me to help you discover new things.'

That wasn't what she had said. Was it? Certainly not in the way she thought he was implying. 'And you think you can do that for me, do you?'

'Maybe.'

She didn't have to see him to know that he was smiling. Anger rose, sharp, hot and a welcome antidote to the sudden intimacy—but she wasn't entirely sure if she was more angry with Gael for his presumption or herself for laying herself open like that. 'How very altruistic of you, and what's in it for you? A better painting or the virtuous glow of helping poor, virginal Hope McKenzie? Sprinkle a little of your privileged, glamorous Upper East Side fairy dust on me and watch me transform? Well, Professor Higgins, this little flower girl doesn't need your patronage, thank you very much.'

'Are you sure about that?' Before she could respond Gael continued smoothly. 'In that case why don't we get started on planning this whirlwind wedding? Any venues you want to see?'

Hope glared at the laptop as if it were to blame for her lack of possibilities. There was no way she wanted to admit she didn't have one idea as yet. 'Yes. Meet me…meet me on top of the Empire State Building in an hour and a half.' Did they do weddings? It almost didn't matter. It was iconic and it was a start.

'On top of the Empire State Building? How romantic. What a shame it isn't Valentine's Day. Am I Cary Grant or Tom Hanks in this scenario?'

'Neither, you're not the hero. You're the wisecracking friend who ends up handcuffed to a stripper on the stag night.'

'I must have missed that scene. Oh, well, there are worse things to be handcuffed to.' And he hung up leaving Hope with a disturbing image involving Gael O'Connor, handcuffs and the red chaise longue. What was more disturbing was the swirl of excitement in her stomach at the very thought...

It was predictably busy at the top of the Empire State Building, the sun and the wind combining to make the walkway uncomfortable in the early afternoon heat, but none of the tourists seemed to be complaining, too busy taking selfies and pointing out landmarks to notice the conditions.

And they would all be tourists. No self-respecting New Yorker would be up here at this time, during the height of the sightseeing buzz. In fact Gael couldn't remember the last time he had set foot up here. It had probably been for a photo shoot—that was why he visited most tourist locations.

Which was a shame because, even hardened local that he was, he had to admit the view was pretty spectacular, the blue of the ocean merging with the blue of the sky and the city rising from the ocean's depths like some mythological Atlantis.

Gael walked around three sides of the viewing platform before he spotted Hope, bright in the same red dress she'd been wearing earlier. She was standing half turned away from him, leaning on the railing staring out over the city, the dark strands of her hair whipping in the wind. It was odd, he'd only met her this morning but her image was indelibly printed on him—probably because most women didn't gatecrash his studio, demand he help them with a wedding and then blurt out their sexual history—or lack of—before nine a.m.

A smile tugged at his lips. He hadn't seen that one coming and at this stage in the game he could have sworn he'd seen it all. Dammit, he had to admit he was intrigued. How old was Hope? He looked at her assessingly. Somewhere in her mid to late twenties, he'd guess. Which meant she had to be either holding out for true love or had a considerable amount of baggage and neither of those things appealed to him. Not that he was interested in Hope in that way. He just needed a model.

She shifted and her full profile came into view. Nice straight nose and a really good mouth—full bottom lip and a lovely shape to the top one. Almost biteable. Almost… 'So, is this it? The perfect spot?'

She jumped as he joined her at the barrier, her cheeks flushing as she threw a stilted smile his way. 'I don't know. It looks a bit busy for a wedding.'

'Which is a good thing because it turns out you can only get married up here on Valentine's Day and only then if you win a competition. I checked…' he added as she raised an enquiring eyebrow. 'They could marry elsewhere and then come up here for photos but to be honest with you Hunter isn't that keen on heights.'

'He isn't?'

'Turns green on the Brooklyn Bridge,' Gael confirmed.

'Why didn't you tell me any of this before I arranged to meet you here?' She turned and glared, hands on her slim hips in what was clearly meant to be an admonishing way. She looked more like a cute pixie.

'And ruin your Deborah Kerr moment? Or are you Meg Ryan? Isn't it every girl's dream to arrange a meeting on the top of the Empire State Building?'

'I already told you, your role is the wisecracking best friend, not the hero.'

'What about your role, Hope? Who are you?' No

woman he knew was content to play the supporting role in their own lives.

'Me? I'm the wedding planner.' She stared out over Manhattan, her face softening. 'Isn't it breathtaking? I can't believe I haven't been up here yet.'

'Seriously? I thought this was the first destination on every tourist's wish list.'

'I'm not exactly a tourist. I live here. Well, for three more months I do. I mean to do the tourist trail at some point but I haven't had a chance yet.' Her voice was wistful.

Not the heroine of her own story, neither a tourist nor a native. If he didn't have a pose in mind he'd paint Hope as something insubstantial, some kind of wandering spirit. 'Why are you here, Hope?'

She turned, blinking in surprise. 'To meet you and make a start on the wedding, why?'

'No, why are you in New York at all? Here you are in the greatest city on earth but you're barely living in it, not experiencing it.'

''I'm planning to.' But her words lacked any real commitment and she looked away. 'But I want a real career, to make something of my life that's about me. All this…' She waved her hand over Manhattan. 'This can wait. It will still be here in ten years' time. I'm here because for the first time in nine years I don't have to worry about anyone but myself. I can put my career and my choices first.'

'Is that what this is? Putting yourself first? Because from where I'm standing you've agreed to all kinds of things you don't want to do for other people. For Brenda, your sister…'

'Brenda's my boss, of course I'm going to do what

she asks me to do. As for Faith, it's complicated. Our parents died when I was eighteen and Faith was only ten. I've raised her. I can't turn my back on her now, not when she needs me, wants me. Besides, she's marrying Hunter in two weeks. She won't be my responsibility any more. This is the last thing I can do for her and I want it to be perfect.' Her mouth wobbled and she swallowed. 'It will be perfect.'

She'd raised her sister? That explained a lot. 'Of course it will. I've agreed to help. Besides, as soon as you mention the Carlyle name any door in the city you want opening will swing open.'

'There's no budget for the wedding at all. Hunter's sending a card. But seriously, what does that even mean? Everyone has some kind of budget.'

Gael couldn't help his grin. It was so long since he'd spoken to someone who didn't live in the rarefied Upper East Side bubble. 'No, not the Carlyles. You've heard people say money's no object?' She nodded, dark eyes fixed on him. 'The Carlyles take that to a whole new level. I have no idea how rich they are but filthy doesn't even begin to cover it.'

'Wow.' She looked slightly stunned. 'And I was worrying that Faith was marrying a street artist with no prospects. I think I was worrying about all the wrong things. I don't think Faith and I are going to fit in with people like that. We're very ordinary.' She hesitated and then turned to him, laying her hand on his forearm. 'Will she be okay? They won't look down on her, will they?'

He might be standing on a platform hundreds of feet up in the air but the air had suddenly got very close. All Gael could feel was that area of skin where Hope's hand lay, all he could smell was the citrus notes of her perfume. He tried to drag his concentration back to the conversation. 'Misty doesn't think like that. She's the least snobby person I've ever met and, believe me, living where I live and doing what I do I have met a *lot* of snobs.' A thought struck him. 'She'll be delighted I'm helping with the wedding. In her head Hunter and I will always be brothers even though he was an annoying three-year-old brat when I moved into their house and we've never hung out in the same circles.' Truth was Hunter had always idolised him. He'd even decided to follow in his footsteps and study art rather than the business degree Misty Carlyle had picked out for her only son.

'She sounds nice, Misty. If she was such a good stepmother then maybe she'll be good for Faith.' Hope's mouth trembled into a poor attempt at a smile. 'Poor Faith has only had me for so long, she deserves a real mother.'

Gael suspected that Misty would be delighted to have a young and pliable daughter-in-law. She still introduced herself as *his* mother even though she'd divorced his dad ten years ago. Still, that was more than his own mother did. 'She is nice,' he conceded. 'By far the best of my parents.'

Hope blinked. 'How many do you have?'

'Are we counting discarded steps? Misty is my father's second ex-wife. My mother was his first. His current wife is number four. We all try and forget about number three.'

Her eyes widened. 'That's a lot of wives.'

'Misty's just divorced husband number five and my mother is on her third marriage.' He shrugged. 'No one in my family takes the whole "as long as you both shall live" part very seriously.'

'My parents met at university, married as soon as they graduated and that was that. I used to think they were really boring. Old before their time, you know? Now I envy them that. That certainty.'

'Oh, my parents are certain every time. I'm not sure if it's more endearing or infuriating, that eternal optimism. They were dancers, Broadway chorus dancers, when they met.'

'No way.'

'Oh, yes,' he said wryly. 'It was very *Forty-Second Street*. Right up to the minute my twenty-year-old dad knocked up my nineteen-year-old mom and carried her back to Long Harbor to the family bar.' His poor young mother, a streetwise Hispanic girl with stars in her eyes, wasn't content with a life serving drinks to the moneyed masses who flocked to the Long Island resort in the summer. 'I don't remember much about that time, but I do remember a lot of yelling. She's Cuban and my dad's Irish so when they fought crockery flew. Literally. Just before my fifth birthday she packed her bags and walked out. Never came back.'

He hadn't realised that he was clenching his fist until Hope's hand covered his, a warm unwanted comfort. He'd shed the last tear he would ever shed on his mother's behalf on his fifth birthday when she'd failed to turn up to her own son's birthday party. 'I'm so sorry. Do you see her now?'

'Occasionally, if I'm near Vegas. She has a dance troupe there, she's doing well but the last thing she needs is a six-foot, twenty-nine-year-old son reminding her that she's nearer fifty than thirty.'

'So you were raised by your dad?'

'And my grandparents, aunts, uncles—anyone else who wanted to tame the wild O'Connor boy. Not that there was much time to run wild, not with a family business like the Harbor Bar—there's always a surface to clean, a table to clear, an errand to run if you're stupid enough to get caught. And Dad wasn't brokenhearted for long. It seemed like there was a whole line of women just dying to become my stepmom. But they all were swept away when Misty decided she was interested. She was fifteen years older than my dad and it was like she was from a different planet. So calm, so together. So one minute I'm that poor motherless O'Connor boy living on top of a bar with a huge extended family, the next I'm rattling around a huge mansion with a monthly allowance bigger than my dad's old salary. It was insane.'

'It sounds like a fairy tale. Like *Cinderella* or something.'

'Fairy tales are strictly a girl thing. It's okay for Cinderella to marry the prince, not so okay for an Irish bartender to marry his way into the upper echelons of society. The more polite people called him a toy boy, but they all wore identical sneers—like they knew exactly what Misty saw in him and didn't think it should be allowed in public. And as for me? Breeding counts, money counts and I had neither. When Dad became Misty Carlyle's third ex-husband then I should have returned to the gutter where I came from.'

By unspoken accord they moved away from the railing and began to walk back to the elevator lobby. 'What happened?

'Misty. She insisted on paying for college, persuaded my dad to let me spend my holidays with her, Christmas skiing, spring break in New York, the summers in Europe. Of course everyone at school knew I was there on charity—not even her stepson any more.' It was hard looking back remembering just how alone he had been, how isolated. They hadn't bullied him; he was too strong for that—and no one wanted to incur Misty's wrath. They had just ignored him. Shown him he was nothing. Until he'd started *Expose* and made them need him.

'That must have been tough.' Her dark eyes were limpid with a sympathy he hadn't asked for and certainly didn't want.

'Expensive education, great allowance and a suite of rooms in one of the oldest and grandest houses in the Hamptons? Yeah, I suffered.' But Gael didn't know if his words fooled Hope. He certainly never managed to fool himself. He greeted the elevator with relief. 'Come on, I'll buy you a coffee and fill you in on everything you need to know about life with the Carlyles. I'll warn you, you may need to take notes. There's a lot to learn.' For Gael as well as Hope. He wasn't entirely sure why he'd decided to go all *This is Your Life* with her but one thing he did know. He wouldn't let his guard down again.

CHAPTER FOUR

'IT'S ALL SET UP and ready to go. Where do you want me to start?' Hope was perched on one achingly trendy and even more achingly uncomfortable high stool, her laptop set up on the kitchen counter, her bright yellow skirt and dotted cream blouse feeling incongruously feminine and delicate set against the stainless steel and matt black cupboards and worktops.

To one side was Gael's own laptop and several backup drives plus a whole box of printed photos, most of which had names and dates pencilled on the back. Hope had spent the morning looking through the box and scanning through a couple of the hard drives before setting up the spreadsheets and database she was planning to use.

Gael strolled into the kitchen carrying yet another box, which he set next to the first. Great. Even more photos. 'I think you are best off starting with the old blog posts. They're all archived and filed.' He pushed one of the hard drives towards her and Hope plugged it into the side of her laptop.

'Okay. So what do you want? Names obviously so we can cross reference them, dates—what else?'

'Any references made to the subjects in *Expose*.

JESSICA GILMORE 55

Once we've finished with that we'll move on to the photos I either didn't use or were taken after the blog closed down. We'll only need names and dates unless they were used professionally in which case the magazine will need referencing as well. Most are saved with all the relevant information but any that aren't put aside into a separate folder and I'll go through them with you at the end of each day.'

She was scribbling fast, taking notes. 'Got it. I don't think it'll take too long. You've kept good notes and everything seems to be labelled...' She hesitated and he looked at her. Really looked at her for the first time since they had left the Empire State Building yesterday afternoon. Oh, she'd spent time with him. Had coffee, learned some tips on handling her new in-laws-to-be, drawn up a list of possible venues for her sister's wedding, but he had retreated behind a shield of courtesy and efficiency. She barely knew him and yet that sudden withdrawal left her feeling lonelier than she had for a long time.

'Everything okay?'

'Yes, it's just... Obviously I know that you're a photographer.'

'Were,' he corrected her. 'Hence the retrospective. I'm a struggling unknown artist now.'

Hope looked around at the kitchen full of gleaming appliances, each worth the same amount as a small car, and repressed a smile. There were few signs of struggling in the studio. '*Were* a photographer. And you do—did—a lot of society shoots and fashion magazines and stuff...'

'And?'

'Where does the blog fit in? If I'm going to cata-

logue properly I need to know what I'm dealing with.'
Somehow Brenda had failed to make this clear in any
one of her excitable emails, most of which just reminded Hope how important this assignment was.

Gael leaned on the counter close beside her. He was
casually clad in dark blue jeans and a loose, short-
sleeved linen shirt. Hope could see every sharply defined muscle in his arms, every dark hair on the olive
skin. '*Expose* was a blog I set up when I was at prep
school. My plan, not surprisingly given the name, was
to expose people. The people I went to school with to
be more precise. I took photos chronicling the misad-
venture of New York's gilded youth. It just skated the
legal side of libellous.' His mouth curved into a provocative smile. 'After all, there was no proof that the
senator's son was *going* to snort that line, that couple
on the table weren't necessarily going to have sex, but
it was implied.' The smile widened. 'Implied because
generally it was true.'

Hope thought back to the hundreds of black and
white photos she had already seen today, stored on hard
drives, in the box, some framed and hung on Gael's
studio walls, the attractive, entitled faces staring out
without a fear in the world. What must it be like to have
that sort of confidence ingrained in you? 'And they let
you just take photos, even when they were misbehaving?' She cursed her choice of word. Misbehaving! She
was living her own stereotype. She'd get out a parasol
next and poke Gael with it, saying, 'Fie! Fie!' like some
twenty-first-century Charlotte Bartlett.

He laughed, a short bitter sound. 'They didn't even
notice. I was invisible at school, which was handy because nobody suspected it was me. They simply didn't

see me.' How was that possible? Surely at sixteen or seventeen he would still have been tall, still imposing, still filling all the space with his sheer presence? 'By the time I was outed as the photographer the blog had become mythic—as had its subjects. To be posted, or even better named and the subject of a post? Guaranteed social success. The papers and gossip magazines began to take an interest in the Upper East Side youth not seen for decades—and it was thanks to me. Instead of being the social pariah I expected to be I found myself the official chronicler of the wannabe young and the damned. That was the end of *Expose*, of course. It limped on through my first years at college but it lost its way when people started *trying* to be in it. I became a society photographer instead as you said, portraits, fashion, big events; lucrative, soulless.'

'But why? Why set it up in the first place? Why run the risk of being caught?' She could understand taking photographs as a way of expressing his loneliness—after all, she had been known to pen the odd angsty poem in her teens. But that was a private thing—thank goodness. She shivered at the very thought of anybody actually *reading* them.

Gael straightened, grey-blue eyes fixed on Hope as if he saw every secret thought and desire. No wonder he'd been so successful if his camera's eye was as shrewd as his own piercing gaze. She swallowed, staring defiantly back as if she were the one painting him, taking him in. But she already knew as much as she was comfortable with. She knew that his hair was cut short but there were hints of a wild, untamed curl, that his eyes were an unexpected grey-blue in the dark, sharply defined face. She knew that he could look at a girl as if he could see inside her. She didn't want to know any more.

'Because I could. Like I say, I was invisible. The people at the schools I went to cared about nothing except your name, your contacts and your trust fund. I had none of the above, ergo I was nothing.' His mouth twisted. 'The arrogance of youth. I wanted to bring them down, show the world how shallow and pathetic the New York aristocracy were. It backfired horribly. The world saw and the world loved them even more. Only now I was part of it for better or for worse. Still am, I suppose. Still, at least it should guarantee interest in the show. Let's just hope the paintings are as successful as the photographs were.'

'But why change? You're obviously really successful at what you do.'

'Fame and fortune have their perks,' he admitted. 'The studio, the invitations, the parties, the money…' the women. He didn't need to say it; the words hung in the humid New York summer air, shimmering in the heat haze. She'd seen the photos: pictures by him, pictures of him—with heiresses, actresses, It Girls and models.

Hope didn't even try to suppress her smirk. 'It must have been very difficult for you.'

'I'm not saying my lifestyle doesn't have its benefits. But it wasn't the way I thought I'd live, the way I wanted to earn a living. *Expose* was just a silly blog, that was all. I thought anyone who saw it would be horrified by the excess, by the sheer waste, but I was wrong.' He shrugged. 'My plan was always art school and then to paint. Somehow I was sidetracked.'

'So this is you getting back on track?'

'Hence the retrospective. Goodbye to that side of my life neatly summed up in an A4 hardback with witty captions. Right, lunch was a little on the meagre side so I'm going to go out and get ice cream. What do you want?'

'Oh.' She looked up, unexpectedly flustered. 'I don't mind.'

He shot her an incredulous look. 'Of course you mind. What if I bought you caramel swirl but really you wanted lemon sorbet? The two are completely different.'

'We usually have cookie dough at home. It's Faith's favourite.' Hope's mind was completely blank. How could she not know which flavour she preferred?

'Great, when I buy Faith an ice cream I'll know what to get. What about you?'

'No, seriously. Whatever you're having. It's fine.' She didn't want this attention, this insistence on a decision, stupid as she knew that made her look. Truth was she had spent so long putting Faith's needs, wants and likes before her own it was a slow and not always comfortable process trying to figure out where her sister ended and she began. 'Thank you.'

Gael didn't answer her smile with one of his own; instead he gave her a hard, assessing look, which seemed to strip her bare, and then turned and left leaving Hope feeling as if she'd failed some kind of test she hadn't even known she was meant to study for.

'Any more? I don't think you tried the double chocolate peanut and popcorn.'

Hope pushed the spoon away and moaned. 'No more, in fact I don't think I can ever eat ice cream again.' She stared at the open tubs, some much less full than others. 'And even after eating all this I don't know which my favourite flavour is.'

'Mint choc,' Gael said. 'That one has nearly gone. Impressive ice-cream-eating skills, Miss McKenzie.'

'If I ever need a reference I'll call you.' She paused and watched Gael as he placed the lids back onto the cartons and stacked them deftly before carrying them to the industrial-sized freezer. She hadn't known what to say, what to think when he'd returned to the studio carrying not one or two but ten different flavours of ice cream.

'You wouldn't pick,' he'd said in explanation as he'd lined the pots up in front of her. A bubble of happiness lodged in her chest. Nobody had ever done anything so thoughtful for her. Maybe she could do this. Work with this man, pose with him, because there were moments when she crossed from wariness to liking.

After all it would be rude not to like someone who bought you several gallons of Italian ice cream.

The pictures on the computer screen blurred in front of her eyes. 'I feel sleepy I ate so much.'

'Then it's a good thing you're about to get some fresh air. There's no time to slack, not with your schedule.'

'Fresh air?'

'Central Park. I spoke to a couple of contacts yesterday and they might just be able to accommodate your sister.'

Central Park! Of course. One of the few iconic New York landmarks she had actually visited and spent time in. Hope obediently slid off her stool, pressing one hand to her full stomach as she did so. She couldn't remember the last time she'd indulged so much. The last time she'd felt free to indulge, not set a good example or worry about what people thought.

Central Park was barely a ten-minute stroll from Gael's studio. Hope had spent several hours wandering around the vast city park but it felt very different walking there with Gael. He clearly knew it intimately, taking her straight to a couple of locations that had availability on Thursday in two weeks' time.

'What do you think?' he asked as they reached the lake. 'Romantic enough or did you prefer the Conservatory Garden?'

'The garden is lovely,' she agreed. 'It's a shame the floral arch is already booked. I think Faith would love it. But with such short notice she'll just have to be grateful we found her anywhere at all.'

'Why on earth is it such short notice? Is it a religious thing? Is that why your sister wants to marry Hunter on six weeks' acquaintance? Why you are still a virgin? You're waiting for marriage? For true love?' She could hear the mockery inherent in the last phrase.

The small bubble of happiness she'd carried since the moment she'd seen the bags heaped with ice cream burst with a short, sharp prick. He thought she was odd, a funny curiosity. 'I don't see that it is any of your business.'

'Hope, tomorrow, or the day after or the day after that, the moment I think you are ready, that you can handle it, you are going to pose for me for a painting which is supposed to symbolise sex. If this is going to work I need to understand why you have made the choices you have. I'm not going to judge you—your body, your decisions. But I need to understand.'

Hope stopped and stared out over the lake, watching a couple in a boat kissing unabashedly, as if they wanted to consume each other. Her stomach tightened. 'Honestly? Is it that unbelievable that a twenty-seven-year-old woman hasn't had sex yet? Does there have to be some big reason?'

'In this day and age, looking like you do? You have to admit it's unusual.' Happiness shivered through her at his casual words. *Looking like you do.* It was hard sometimes to remember a time when she had felt like someone desirable, bursting with promise and confidence, confident in her teeny shorts and tight tops as only an eighteen-year-old girl could be.

'It's no big mystery. It's not like I have been saving myself for my knight in shining armour.' She didn't believe in him for one thing. 'It just happened.' Hope turned away from the lake, dragging her eyes away from the oblivious, still-snogging couple with difficulty. For the first time in a really long time she allowed herself to wish it were her. Oblivious to everything but the sun on her back, the gentle splash of the water, his smell, his taste, the feel of his back under her hands. She had no idea who 'he' was but she ached for him nonetheless.

'I told you I raised Faith after our parents died. My aunt offered to help. She had a couple of kids Faith's age and would have been happy to have had her. But I wanted her to grow up where I grew up, in the family house, stay at her school with her friends.' She twisted her hands together. It all sounded so reasonable when she said it but there had been nothing reasonable about her decision at the time. Just high emotion, bitter grief and desperate guilt.

'So you put everything on hold?' He sounded disbelieving and she couldn't blame him; it sounded crazy said so bluntly. But she had had no real choice—not that she wanted to tell him that. To let him know she was responsible for it all. She had to take care of Faith—if it wasn't for Hope she would have had her family intact.

She swallowed, the old and familiar guilt bitter on her tongue. 'I didn't mind. But it meant my life was so different from my friends' new worlds—they were worrying about boyfriends and exams and going out and I was worrying about paying bills and childcare. It was no wonder we drifted apart. My boyfriend went to university just a few weeks after the funeral and I knew it would be best to end it then, that I wouldn't be able to put anyone else first for a long time.' It had seemed like the logical thing to do but she had hoped that he would fight for her, just a little.

But he had disappeared off without a word. He was getting married in just a few short weeks, his life moving on seamlessly from grungy teen to pretentious student to a man with responsibilities, just the way it was supposed to. Just as hers was supposed to have done.

Gael was like a dog with a bone. 'Let me get this straight: you didn't date at all? Since you were eighteen you have been single?'

How could she explain it? It all sounded so drab and dreary—and in many ways it had been. Those first few years when she earned so little, the long nights in alone while Faith slept, studying for her Open University degree, the ever-widening chasm between herself and her school friends until the day she realised she had no one to confide in. Too young for the mums at the school gates and the other secretaries at her law firm, too old at heart and shackled by responsibilities for the few girls around her age she managed to meet.

And then there was the rest: the lack of money or time to take care of herself and the slow dawning realisation she had lost any sense of style or joy in clothes and hair. It was hard when she had no budget to indulge herself and little time or talent to make the most of what she could afford. But there had been other things that compensated—watching Faith star in her school play, taking her ice skating at Somerset House, organising sleepovers and pamper evenings and home-made pizza parties for her sister and her friends and seeing her sister shine with happiness. Surely that was worth any sacrifice?

'No, I dated. A little. But I didn't like to stay out late, even when Faith was older and no one could stay over, it didn't seem right. And so the few relationships I had never really went anywhere. It's really no big deal.'

'Okay,' but she could hear the scepticism. Hope didn't blame him. How could she fool him when she had forgotten how to fool herself? 'Come on.'

Gael took her arm and turned her down a path on their left, his walk determined and his eyes gleaming with a devilish glint she instinctively both distrusted and yearned for. 'Where are we going?'

He stopped in front of a red and yellow brick hexagon and grinned at her. 'When's the last time you rode on a carousel, Hope?'

Was he mad? He *must* be mad. Hope stared over at the huge carousel. It was like a step back in time, wooden horses, their mouths fixed open, heads always thrown up in ecstasy, their painted manes blowing in a non-existent breeze as the circular structure turned to the sound of a stately polka. 'I don't know when I last rode on one,' she said and that was true. She couldn't pinpoint the date but she knew it was before Faith was born. Before she had elected to opt out of family life. She vividly remembered standing by the side of a carousel in the park as her parents took her laughing baby sister on one. She had refused to accompany them, had said it was too babyish. Instead she had stood by the side feeling left out and unloved, hating them for respecting her word and not forcing her to ride.

'You'll always be able to answer that question from now on. The eighteenth of August, you can say confidently. In New York, around...' He squinted at his wrist. 'Around two-forty in the afternoon.'

'No, I can say the eighteenth of August is the day some crazy person tried to persuade me to go on one and I walked away.' She swivelled, ready to turn away, only to be arrested by a hand closing gently around her wrist. She glared at Gael scornfully. 'What, you're going to force me to go on?'

'No, of course not.' He sounded bemused and who could blame him? She was acting crazy. But she could still see them, the two forty-somethings cradling their precious toddler tight while their oldest child stood forgotten by the exit.

Only she hadn't been forgotten. They had waved every time they passed by, every time. No matter that she hadn't waved back once. Hope swallowed, the lump in her throat as painful as it was sudden. Why hadn't she waved?

Gael leaned in close, his fingers still loose around her wrist. His breath was faint on her neck but she could sense every nerve where it touched her, each one shocking her into awareness. 'Doesn't it look like fun?'

Maybe, maybe not. 'I'll look ridiculous.'

'Will you? Do they? Look at them, Hope.'

Hope raised her eyes, her skin still tingling from his nearness, a traitorous urge to lean back into him gripping her. *Stop it*, she scolded herself. *You've known him for what? Two days? And he's already persuaded you to pose nude, holds your career in his rather nicely shaped hands and is trying to make a fool of you. There's no need to help him by swooning into him.*

But now he was so close she could smell him, a slight scent of linseed and citrus, not unpleasant but unusual. It was the same scent she had picked up in his studio. A working scent. He might be immaculately dressed in light grey trousers and a white linen shirt but the scent told her that this was a man who used his hands, a physical being. The knowledge shivered through her, heating as it travelled through her veins.

'Hope?'

'Yes, I'm looking at them.' She wasn't lying, she was managing somehow to push all thoughts about Gael O'Connor's hands out of her mind and focus on the carousel, on the people riding it. Families, of course. The old pain pierced her heart at the sight; time never seemed to dull it, to ease it.

But it wasn't just families riding; there were groups of older children, laughing hysterically, a couple of teens revelling in the irony of their childish behaviour. Couples, including a white-haired man, stately on his golden steed, smiling at the silver-haired woman next to him. 'No,' she admitted. 'They don't look ridiculous. They look like they are having fun.'

'Well, then,' and before she could formulate any further response or process what was happening she was at the entrance of the building and Gael was handing over money in crisp dollar bills.

'Go on, pick one,' he urged and she complied, choosing a magnificent-looking bay with a black mane and a delicate high step. Gael swung himself onto the white horse next to hers while Hope self-consciously pulled her skirt down and held on to the pole tightly. He looked so at ease, as if he came here and did this every day, one hand carelessly looped round the pole, the other holding a small camera he had dug out of his jeans pocket.

'Smile!'

'What are you doing?'

He raised an eyebrow. 'Practising my trade. Watch out, it's about to go. Hold on tight!'

The organ music swelled around them as the carousel began to rotate and the horses moved, slowly at first, before picking up speed until it was whirling around and around. At first Hope clung on tightly, afraid she might fall as the world spun giddily past, but once she settled into the rhythm she relaxed her grip. Gael was right, it was fun. More than that, it was exhilarating, the breeze a welcome change on the hot, sticky day. Above the organ music she could hear laughter, children, adults and teens, all forgetting their cares for one brief whirl out of time. She risked a glance at Gael. He was leaning back, nonchalant and relaxed, like a cowboy in total control of his body; his balance, his hand was steady as he focussed the camera and snapped again and again, watching the world through a lens.

And then all too soon it was slowing, the walls

slowly coming back into focus, the horse no longer galloping but walking staidly along as the music died down. She looked over at Gael and smiled shakily, unable to find the words to thank him. For a moment then she had been free. No one's sister, no one's PA, no expectations. Free.

'Another go?'

'No, thank you, one was enough. But it *was* fun. You were right.'

'Remember that over the next two weeks and we'll be fine.' Gael dismounted in one graceful leap, holding a hand out so that Hope could try and slide down without her skirt riding up too far. 'Come on, let's have a drink at the Tavern on the Green and you can decide if you like it enough to shortlist it for the wedding drinks.'

'Good idea.' Damn, why hadn't she thought of that? Celebrating her sister's wedding in such an iconic venue would certainly be memorable.

Hope stopped, suddenly shy, trying to find the right words to frame the question that had been dogging her thoughts since their conversation at the lake. 'Gael, when will I be ready? To be painted?'

It wasn't that she felt ready; she wasn't sure she ever would be. But knowing that at some point it would happen, at some point she would have to keep her word, made it almost possible for her to relax.

Gael didn't answer for a moment, just stared at her with that intense, soul-stripping look that left her feeling as if she had nowhere left to hide.

'When you start living,' he said and turned and walked away. Hope stood still, gaping at him.

'I am ready,' she wanted to yell. Or, 'Then you'll be waiting a long time.' Because the truth was she was scared. Scared of what would happen, scared of who she was, scared of what might be unleashed if she ever dared to let go.

CHAPTER FIVE

HOPE STOOD IN her walk-in wardrobe and stared at the rack of carefully ironed clothes, fighting back almost overwhelming panic. Panic and, she had to admit, a tinge of anticipation. Every day for the last nine years had followed its own dreary predictable pattern and even here, in the vibrant Upper East Side, she had managed to re-establish a set routine before she'd worked out the best place to buy milk.

But not today. She had no idea what Gael had in store for her. He'd told her to be ready at ten a.m. and that he would call for her. Nothing else.

He'd mentioned risks. Allowing herself to live. Unlocking herself. Hope swallowed. She liked the sound of that, she really did. She just wasn't sure whether it was possible, that if she stripped away the layers of self-sufficiency and efficiency and busyness there would be very much left.

'Okay,' she said aloud, the words steadying her. 'What's the worst that could happen?'

Oh. She shouldn't have even thought that because now, now she had opened up the floodgates, it turned out she could think of *lots* of worst things. Maybe he was going to suggest skydiving or bungee jumping off the Brooklyn Bridge—illegal but even Hope had heard the rumours and she bet Gael O'Connor didn't give two figs for legality anyway. Or climbing up some skyscraper—or walking a tightrope between them. She inhaled shakily. No, she was pretty sure she could strike the last one off her list.

Or maybe when he said he wanted her to loosen up he was talking about her V card. He might be a member of one of those exclusive clubs where expensive call girls and even more expensive cigars and whisky were shared by men in ten-thousand-dollar suits. Possibly. She'd seen a TV show once where the detective went undercover in exactly that kind of club right here in New York City...

Or maybe he would want her to explore her own sexuality in a burlesque class or pole dancing or actually perform in some kind of club or...or no. Ten minutes would be nine minutes and fifty nine seconds longer than she needed to convince any stage manager that she most definitely didn't have what it took. After all, how many four-year-olds were asked to leave baby ballet?

'Stop thinking.' Hope grabbed a pair of high-waisted orange shorts and a cream *broderie-anglaise* blouse and marched out of the wardrobe, throwing them onto the daybed, which doubled as a sofa and place to sleep. Living in a studio so compact it practically redefined the word had meant she needed to find new levels of neatness and organisation or resign herself to living surrounded by everything she had brought with her in disordered chaos. And that, obviously, would be intolerable.

Dressed, her hair brushed and tied back into a high ponytail, and her feet encased in a comfortable pair

of cream and tan summer loafers, she should, she re-
flected, have felt better. That was what her new, eye-
wateringly expensive wardrobe was supposed to do.
Make her feel ready for anything. Make her feel like
someone. Instead she felt all too often like a little girl
playing dress up in the bold colours, designs and cuts.
Maybe she should get changed…

Right on cue, as if Gael knew the exact moment she
was feeling the most insecure, the buzzer went. No
doorman here, no lift or fancy hallway. Just a buzzer
and several flights of stairs.

Not that the four flights of stairs seemed to faze him.
He was annoyingly cool when she opened the door,
his breathing regular, not a damp patch to be seen on
the grey short-sleeved shirt he'd teamed with a pair of
well-cut black jeans. His clothes gave no clue to the
day's activities although she could probably rule out
the gentleman's club. Her eyes met his and, as she took
in the lurking laughter, all the calm, welcoming words
she had prepared and practised fell away.

'Do you want to get going?'

He took a step forward until he was standing just
inside her threshold. 'Are you in a hurry? It's usually
considered polite to invite a guest in. Or is there something you don't want me to see?'

As if. Her life was an open book. A very dull book,
which had been left to gather dust on the library shelf,
a little like her. 'Not at all. I just thought you might
want to get started. Ah, come in. Although you are. In.'

How had he done that? Eased himself in through the
door and past her so smoothly she had barely noticed.
She should add magician to his list of talents.

Come on, Hope, get some control. 'Tea?' When in doubt revert to a good national stereotype.

'Iced?'

'No, the normal kind. I have Earl Grey, normal, Darjeeling and peppermint.'

His mouth quirked. 'Seriously?'

'Er…yes. I found this little shop which sells imported British goods and I stocked up…' *Stop talking right now, Hope.* But her mouth didn't get the message. 'Tea and pickle, sandwich pickle, not gherkins. And real chocolate, no offence. There's many things the US does better, like coffee and cheesecake, but I would give my firstborn for a really mature cheddar cheese and pickle sandwich followed by a proper chocolate bar.'

Just in case he had any doubt she was socially awkward she was spelling it out for him loud and clear. She hadn't always been this way; if only she could turn the clocks back nine years—although if it was a choice between getting her confidence back or her parents there was no contest. She'd happily be awkward for ever.

Mercifully Gael didn't pursue the conversation. He stood in the middle of the room, dominating all the space in the tiny studio. 'Nice address.'

'Location is everything. Apparently it makes up for the lack of actual space—at least that's what Maddison says. It's her apartment,' she explained as his eyebrows shot up in query. 'We swapped homes when we swapped jobs.' Not that Maddison was currently occupying either Hope's home or her job; instead she was cosied up in the home of Hope's old boss, Kit Buchanan, planning a future together. Hope had worked with Kit for three years and he had never stepped even a centimetre over the professional line but barely a couple of months with Maddison and he had given up his job and was planning a whole new life with the American. Hope couldn't help wondering how the job swap had turned Maddison's life so radically upside down while hers was left untouched.

And look at Faith. Less than three months into her travels and she was engaged to the heir to a multimillion-dollar fortune, which was an awful lot more than most people managed on a gap year. What had Hope done in the city that never slept? Tried a few new bagel flavours and experimented with her coffee order. Hold the front page.

Maybe today wasn't going to be so horrendous after all. Whatever Gael had planned at least it would be *new*. Maybe this was all for the best—what was the point in bemoaning the dullness of her life if she didn't grasp this chance to shake things up a little?

Gael strolled over to the window in just four long strides. 'I like it. Nice light.' The apartment didn't compare with his, of course, but thanks to the gorgeous bay window the light did flood in, bathing the white room with an amber glow. The window opened far enough for Hope to climb out onto the fire escape so she could perch on the iron staircase, cup of tea in one hand, book in the other, soaking up the sunshine.

'It does for me. I don't need much space.' Which was a good thing. A tiny table and solitary chair sat in the bay of the window, the daybed occupied the one spare wall lying opposite the beautiful and incongruously large fireplace. The kitchen area—two cupboards and a two-ring stove—took up the corner by the apartment door and a second door to its right led into the walk-in closet equipped with rails and drawers, which opened directly into the diminutive but surprisingly well appointed bathroom. Two people in the studio would be cosy, three a crowd, but this was the first time Hope had shared the space with anyone else. Unless she counted the Skype conversations with her sister.

Loneliness slammed into her, almost knocking the breath out of her.

Gael's mouth quirked into a knowing smile. 'I'm sure you don't. More used to accommodating others than demanding space, aren't you?'

'There's nothing wrong with being able to live simply. What do I need? For today? A coat? Different shoes?' She wasn't going to ask what they were doing, show any curiosity, but she wasn't above digging for a clue.

Gael turned and looked her over slowly and deliberately. It was an objective look, similar to the way he'd looked at her when he asked to paint her, as if she were an object, not a living, breathing person and certainly not as if she was a woman or in any way desirable. And yet her nerves smouldered under his gaze as if the long-buried embers remembered what it felt like to blaze free.

'You'll do as you are.' That was a fat lot of help.

'Great.' Hope grabbed her bag. 'Lead on, then. The sooner we get this over with, the sooner I can get on with some wedding planning for Faith. Don't think I'm here for any other reason.'

But even as she said the words Hope knew she wasn't being entirely honest, not with him, not with herself. She could tell herself as much as she liked that she was only spending time with Gael for her sister, for her job. But the truth was she needed a way out of the rigid constraints and fears she had built around her. And whatever happened over the next two weeks or so Hope knew that she would be changed in some way. And that had to be a good thing, didn't it? Because this life swap had shown her that it wasn't her old job, or raising Faith or living in her childhood house that had imprisoned her. It was Hope herself. Which meant there was no handsome prince or fairy godmother waiting in the wings to transform her life, to transform her.

This was her chance and she was going to grab it.

'So, where exactly are we going? Do we need to get a cab?' Hope was trying to sound nonchalant but Gael could tell that she was eaten up with curiosity. What had she been imagining? Probably the worst—after all, hadn't he told her that he wanted her to take some risks? To start living? She'd probably put those remarks together with the paintings and come up with some seduction scenario straight out of a nineteen-seventies porn movie.

But it wasn't her body he needed to start exploring, no, not even in those shorts, which hugged her compact body perfectly, lengthening her legs and rounding nicely over what was a very nice bottom. He had never deflowered a virgin, not even in his school days, and had no intention of starting now. Inexperience physically meant inexperience emotionally and Gael had no intention of dealing with crushes or infatuation or anything else equally messy. No matter how enticing the package.

Hang on—when had Hope gone from convenient minion and model to enticing? He'd been so busy with the exhibition he'd been living like a monk for the last few months—which was more than a little ironic, considering how much naked female flesh had been on display in his studio. It wasn't *her* per se. No, Hope was just the first woman he had spent any time with in a social capacity in a while. Obviously boundaries would blur a little.

Not that this was really social. Sort out the wedding, crack open that shell she'd erected around herself and she'd be ready for him to paint. That was why he was here, why he'd spent yesterday afternoon wandering around Central Park encouraging her to forget her dignity and enjoy the carousel ride. At the end of the day it was all business.

And he refused to dwell on just how enjoyable the business had ended up being... 'No cab needed. It's just a few blocks.'

'Okay.'

She still sounded apprehensive and Gael's conscience gave him a small but definite nudge. His skill, talent aside, had always been to put people at their ease, so much so that they almost forgot he was there. That was how he managed to take so many fly-on-the-wall photos; no paparazzi tricks for him. No, just the ability to blend in, to become part of the furniture. But something about Hope McKenzie had him rubbed up all the wrong way; he liked seeing her bristle a little too much, couldn't resist winding her up. But a brittle, wary subject wasn't going to give him the kind of picture he needed. It was time to turn up the charm. 'We're going to the Metropolitan Museum of Art. I want you to look at an original Manet and some portraits to get an idea of what I want from you—and then we can look at the roof terrace. It's beautiful up there and you might want to consider it for the reception. They don't usually hire it out but I might be able to pull some strings.'

'That sounds great.'

Gael repressed a grin as Hope exhaled a very audible sigh of relief. 'What, did you think I was going to send you on some kind of Seduction 101 course? Starting with the dance of the seven veils and ending up in some discreet bordello?'

'Of course not,' but the colour in her cheeks belied her words. Interesting, her imagination had definitely been at play. Had he figured in it at all? The seducer, the cad, the lover? The architect, leading her through her seductive education? Gael tore his mind back to the matter at hand, refusing to allow it to dwell on the interesting scenes so effortlessly conjured up.

He stopped as Hope halted at a snack stand to pick up a bottle of water and an apple. She turned, the apple in one hand, like Eve tempting him to fall. 'Would you like anything?'

'No, thanks.' He'd forgotten that girls, that women, did that. Bought their own water, a normal bottle of water from a normal silver metal snack stand just outside Central Park. The women he dated demanded fancy delis and even fancier water imported from remote places with prices to match.

And they never paid their way. Hope hadn't even sent him a hopeful sideways look; instead she'd offered to treat him. To water and a piece of fruit, but still. It was a novel experience—and not a displeasing one.

'So.' She had sunk her teeth into the apple, juice on her lips. He tried not to stare, not to be too fascinated by the glistening sweetness, but his eyes were drawn back to the tempting plumpness. The serpent knew what it was doing when it selected an apple; Adam had never stood a chance. 'Do we have to go into special rooms to look at the paintings or are they respectable nudes?'

'It's all perfectly respectable,' he promised as they turned the corner and walked towards the steps leading up to the arched entrances of the museum. As usual the steps were crowded: groups of girls gossiping while sipping from huge coffee cups, lone people scrolling through phones, sketching or reading battered paperbacks, couples entwined and picnicking families. The usual sense of coming home washed over him. The museum had been a sanctuary when he had lived in Misty's town house, the place he had come to on exeats from school. The only place where he had felt that he knew who he was. Where his anonymity wasn't a curse but a blessing as he moved through the galleries, just another tourist.

Hope tossed her apple core into a trash can and wiped her hands on a tissue before lobbing that in after her apple. 'I pass this every day on my way to work,' she said as they began to climb the stairs. 'I always meant to come in.'

'What stopped you? It's open late and at weekends.'

Hope shrugged. 'I don't know, the usual, I suppose.'

'Which is?'

'That because I haven't before I don't know how to. And before you say anything, yes, I know it's stupid. But even though we lived in London my parents weren't really museum people or theatre people—they were far more likely to take us for a walk. They liked nothing better than driving out to a hill somewhere so we could walk up it and eat sandwiches in the drizzle. It was always drizzling!'

'My parents didn't take me to museums either—Misty's interest only runs to showing off her philanthropy and my dad only stepped foot inside when it was the annual ball and only then under duress. I think that's why I loved it so much; it's somewhere I discovered for myself. What did you do as a teenager?'

'Hung out with friends, the usual.' But her voice was constrained and she had turned a little away from him, a clear sign she didn't want to talk about it.

They reached the doors and entered the magnificent Great Hall with its huge ceilings and sweeping arches. Gael palmed his pass, steering Hope past the queues waiting patiently to check their bags in and pay for admittance until he reached the membership desk.

The neatly dressed woman behind the desk smiled, barely looking at his pass. 'Good morning, Mr O'Connor. Is this young lady your guest?'

'Good morning, Jenny. How's the degree going? Yes, Hope's with me.'

'First-name terms with the staff?' Hope murmured as he led her down the corridor, expertly winding his way around tour groups and puzzled clumps of map-wielding visitors.

'I may come here fairly regularly.' Plus he was a patron—and Misty sat on the prestigious Board of Trustees but Hope didn't need to know that. He didn't want to dazzle her with his connections; he'd learned long ago that women impressed with those were only after one thing—influence. He'd vowed long ago never to be used again. He might be enjoying Hope's company but, just like every other woman, she was with him because of what he could do for her. It was a lesson he was unlikely to forget.

Hope sank onto the couch with a grateful cry. 'I wore my most comfortable shoes and *still* my feet ache. We must have walked miles and miles and miles without ever going outside. And my eyes ache just as much as my feet.'

Gael suppressed a smile. 'It's not easy compressing two thousand plus years of art history into a four-hour tour.'

'Five hours and only a twenty-minute coffee stop,' Hope said bitterly. 'I almost fainted away right in front of the Renoir—or was it Degas?'

'Better get it right or you'll fail the written test later. I've ordered a cheese plate, water and a glass of wine. Do you think that will fortify you?'

'Only if I don't have to move again. Ever.'

'Not for the next half hour,' Gael promised. 'But then we have a private tour of the roof garden and the Terrace Room. Your sister can't get married here but she can certainly have the reception. Do you know how many you're organising it for yet?'

Hope rubbed her temples. 'Not exactly but because Misty is planning such a lavish party and a blessing two days later the wedding day itself is to be kept small and intimate. Last email she said that she would like to keep it down to me, you, Hunter's mother of course. His father—will that be awkward in such a small group?'

'I don't think so. Misty and he still move in all the same circles. I told you yesterday, she specialises in civilised divorces.'

'Then a couple of the groom's friends and apparently they are paying for two of Faith's school friends and our aunt and her family to fly over. So that will be...' she totted up the amount on her fingers '...fifteen.'

'Hmm, we might rattle around a bit in the Terrace Room. Let's have a look and see what you think.'

'Faith emailed yesterday to say she would definitely like to have two dresses, which is great because finding just one isn't proving to be at all awkward. Something subtle for the wedding because it's so small, but I think she wants to go all out for the party, especially as they will be repeating their vows.' Hope bit her lip. 'It's such a responsibility. The couple of places I spoke to yesterday seemed to imply that it was easier to learn to do heart surgery in a fortnight than it is to buy and fit a wedding dress. And it's not just the dress. There's a veil, tiara, jewellery. Underwear. And she wants me to sort out bridesmaids' dresses for just me for the ceremony but for both friends and our cousin for the party as well.'

Gael got that Hope felt responsible for her sister, that she had raised her. But this amount of stress all for someone else? He couldn't imagine a single member of his family—including all the exes and steps—putting themselves out for someone else. He had them all on the list for his exhibition's opening-night party and knew Misty would be there if she possibly could. His father if there was nothing better to do. But his mother? She hadn't made his graduation from school or college, he doubted she'd make the effort for a mere party. Funny how, much as he told himself he didn't care, her casual desertion still stung after all these years—only he was so used to it that it was more of a pinprick than anything really wounding.

He didn't know if it was better or worse that she adored his two half-brothers so much, every occasional email a glowing testimonial to their unique specialness. No, he might still have two living, breathing parents but Faith was luckier than he was. What would it be like to have someone like Hope on your side? Someone you could count on? 'You could say no. Ask her to come and organise it herself.'

But she was already shaking her head. 'No. I promised her that I would take care of everything. If things were different she'd have a mother to help her. Well, she doesn't, she only has me. I won't let her down.' There was a telltale glimmer in her eyes and her words caught as she spoke. She looked away, swallowing convulsively as the waitress brought their food and drink over.

Gael sat back, smiling his thanks as the waitress placed their drinks and the cheese platter onto the table. Hope swallowed again and he gave her a moment to compose herself, glad that it was so quiet in the members' only lounge he had brought her to. 'What about you, Hope? Who takes care of you?'

She stared at him, her eyes wide in her pale face. 'I take care of me. I always have.'

'And you're doing just fine, is that what you're saying? You don't know how to step out of your limited comfort zone. You pour all your energy into work and looking after your sister and you're lonely. But you don't need anyone. Sure. You keep telling yourself that.'

What was he saying? He was all about the self-sufficiency himself. But it was different for him. He was toughened whereas Hope was like a toasted marshmallow—a superficial hardened edge hiding an utter mess on the inside. He'd only known her for less than three days but he'd diagnosed that within the first day. And it was a shame. She was a trier…that was evident. She cared, maybe a little too much. A girl like that should have someone to look out for her.

'Thanks for the diagnosis, Doc.' Hope picked up her wine glass and held it up to him in a toast. 'I'll make sure I come to you every time I need relationship advice. Especially as I spent a lot of time yesterday looking through photos at your place and do you know what I didn't see? I didn't see a single photo of you having fun. Oh, yes…' as he tried to interrupt. 'There are pictures of you posing next to women. Sometimes you have your arm around their waist. But you never look like you're enjoying yourself, you never look relaxed. You're as alone as I am—more so. I have Faith. Hunter said you were his brother but you were very quick to deny any relationship with him at all.'

Touché. Gael clinked her glass with his own. 'But I prefer to be by myself. It's my choice. Is it yours, or are you just too afraid to let anyone in? Either way, here's to Hunter and Faith, getting their wedding and this painting out of the way and returning to our solitary lives. Cheers.'

CHAPTER SIX

WHAT WAS IT about Gael O'Connor that made her bristle like an outraged cat? Hope usually hid her feelings so well sometimes it seemed, even to her, that she didn't have any. Slights, slurs and digs passed her by. It didn't rankle when the girls at work went out without her, when they chatted about nights out in front of her as if she weren't even there. She barely noticed when photos of school reunions she hadn't been invited to showed up on her social-media pages or when wedding photos were circulated and she wasn't amongst the guests. Hope had chosen to remove herself from the human race, had chosen to devote herself and her life to Faith; she wasn't going to complain now her job was almost done.

Why would she when she had raised a happy, confident, bright girl who had her whole future before her? She could never fully make things up to her little sister but she had done as much as was humanly possible—and if she had sacrificed her own life for that, well, that felt like a fair trade. She was at peace with her decision.

At peace until Gael opened his mouth, that was. As soon as that mocking note hit his voice her hackles rose and she responded every single time. Was it because he didn't care for the official 'Hope is wonderful to give everything up for Faith' line, instead making her sound like a pathetic martyr living life vicariously instead of in reality? She didn't need it pointed out. She knew she wasn't wonderful or selfless but she didn't feel like a martyr. Usually.

Still, she couldn't complain too much when in one afternoon he had managed to sort out the wedding venues and in such smooth style. It helped that they were looking at a Thursday afternoon wedding and not the weekend but Gael had known all the right people to talk to, to ensure the tight timescales weren't a problem. After consulting with the blissful and all too absent couple they had decided to hold the ceremony in Central Park itself, at a beautiful little leafy spot by the lake, followed by cocktails at the Tavern on the Green. The Met's Roof Garden closed to the public at four-thirty p.m. and wasn't usually available for private hire, but Gael had managed to sweet talk the event coordinator into letting them in after hours for drinks and dinner. So all Hope needed to do was organise afternoon entertainment, evening entertainment, flowers and clothes. She still had just over ten days. Easy.

Now all she wanted to do was fling herself onto the surprisingly comfortable daybed and sleep for at least twelve hours. Her feet still throbbed from the whistle-stop tour through the history of art and her head was even worse. But sleep was a long, long way away. Instead she had less than an hour to shower and get ready. 'I'll pick you up at eight,' Gael had said brusquely as they'd finalised the details with first the event organiser at the Met and then with the Central Park authorities. 'It might be worth eating first.'

Okay. This wasn't a date. Obviously. It was part work, part family business but still. Hope would bet her half of her overpriced London home that not one of the beauties she had seen hanging off Gael's arm in photos had ever taken less than three hours to get ready—and he would have always bought them dinner.

She crammed the rest of her Pop-Tart into her mouth and grabbed a banana reasoning that the addition of fruit turned her snack into a balanced meal.

Thirty minutes later she was showered with freshly washed and dried hair and dressed in one of her new dresses. She hadn't dared wear it before, much as she liked the delicate coffee-coloured silk edged with black lace; it was just so short, almost more of a tunic than a dress... She fingered a pair of thick black tights; surely they would make the dress more respectable? But it was still so hot and humid and her own legs were the brownest they had ever been thanks to weekends spent reading on her fire escape. Hope stared down at what seemed like endless naked flesh before cramming her feet into a pair of black and cream sandals she'd bought on sale but not yet worn because she wasn't entirely sure she could walk in them.

Hope steeled herself to look in the mirror. It was like looking at a stranger: a girl with huge eyes, emphasised with liquid liner and mascara, hair swept back into a low, messy bun, tendrils hanging around her face. This girl looked as if she belonged on the Upper East Side; she looked ready for anything. This girl was an imposter but maybe, just maybe, she could exist for a night or two.

The sound of the buzzer brought her back to the room, to the evening ahead, and Hope blinked a couple of times, getting her bearings back, returning to reality. Rather than buzz Gael up she grabbed her bag and slowly, teetering slightly as she adjusted to the height of the shoes, made her way out of the studio and down the stairs into the evening heat.

Gael took one look at her feet and hailed a cab, much to Hope's relief. She breathed a deep sigh of satisfaction as she sank into the back seat and swapped the evening humidity for the bliss of air conditioning. She had spent twenty-seven years in London considering air conditioning a seldom-needed luxury—less than a day in the New York summer and she'd changed her tune for ever.

She didn't recognise the address Gael gave the cab driver and so sat back, none the wiser about her destination, watching the streets of Manhattan slide slowly past. They were heading west and down, towards the busy tourist hotspots of Times Square and Broadway. She lived barely half an hour's walk from the lively theatre district and yet had only visited once, quickly defeated by the crowds and the heat. Hope stared out of the cab window at the crowded streets thronged with an eclectic mix of tourists, locals and hustlers—the busiest district of New York City by far.

The cab made its slow progression along Fifty-First Street until just after the road intersected with Broadway and then pulled up outside a small, dingy-looking theatre. Hope hadn't been entirely sure what to expect but it wasn't this down-at-heel-looking place. She pulled the dress down as she got out of the cab, wishing she had worn the black tights, feeling both overexposed and overdressed. Gael took her arm. 'This way.' They were the first words he had said to her all evening.

He ushered her through the wooden swing door into the lobby. It was a study in faded glory: old wooden panelling ornately carved and in need of a good dust, the red carpet faded and threadbare in places. It was the last place she had expected Gael to bring her. He was smart in a pale grey suit, his hair sleeked down, as incongruous a contrast to the tatty surroundings as she was. He handed two tickets to a woman dressed like a nineteen-forties usherette and then led Hope down the corridor into the theatre.

It was like stepping into another world. The huge chandeliers hanging from the high ceiling gave out a warm, dim glow, bathing the gold-leafed auditorium in flattering lowlights. The seats had been removed from the stalls and instead it was set up cabaret style with round tables for two, four or six taking up the floor space instead. Many tables were full already, their laughing, chattering occupants wearing anything from jeans to cocktail dresses.

The stage was set up with a microphone and a comfortable-looking leather chair. Nothing else. Steps led up from the floor to the stage.

Gael led her to a small table with just two chairs near the front, pulling a chair out for her with exaggerated courtesy. 'Two glasses of Pinot Noir, please,' he said to the hovering waitress, who was also dressed in nineteen-forties garb. Hope opened her mouth to change the order, she preferred white wine to red, especially on a hot night like this, but she closed it again as the waitress walked away, not caring enough to call the woman back.

'What is this?' she asked as she took her seat. 'Are you thinking this will be suitable entertainment for after the wedding meal?'

'What? Oh, no. We're looking into that later. Right now, this is all about you.' The wolfish look in his eyes did nothing to reassure her and she took the glass the waitress handed her with a mechanical smile. This wasn't some kind of comedy improvisation place, was it? Oh, no, what if it was audience participation? She would rather dance in public than try and tell jokes. And she'd probably prefer to strip naked rather than dance. Maybe that was the point.

Just as she tried to formulate her next question the lights dimmed and one lone spotlight lit up the chair and the microphone. The buzz of conversation quietened as, with an audible scrape and squeak, all chairs turned to face the stage. It remained empty for what was probably less than a minute but felt longer as the anticipation built, the air thick with it. Hope clasped her glass, her stomach knotted. She doubted she was here to see an avant-garde staging of Shakespeare or some minimalist musical.

Finally, a low drum roll reverberated throughout the room, the low rumble thrumming in her chest as if it were part of her heartbeat, and a woman stepped out onto the stage. She was tall, strikingly dressed in a floor-length black dress, a top hat incongruously perched on her head.

'Good evening, ladies and gentlemen, I am delighted to welcome you to the Hall of Truth tonight. As you know the entertainment is you and the stage is yours. This is where you are able to free yourselves of an unwanted burden. You are welcome to share anything—a secret, something humorous, a sad tale, a confession, a rant, a declaration, anything you like. Here are the rules: what's said in the Hall of Truth stays in the Hall of Truth unless it's illegal—there's no confessor's bond here, people.' A nervous laugh at this as people turned in their seats as if searching out any potential villain.

The blonde Master of Ceremonies smiled as the laugh faded away. 'No slander, no judgement and—most importantly—no lies. And no singing or dancing. There are no directors here searching out their next star! Oh, and please switch your cell phones off. Anyone caught recording or videoing will be prosecuted and, besides, it's bad manners. Okay. As is customary on these occasions I'll start. Anyone who would like to contribute please let a waitress know and you'll be added to tonight's set list.' She took in a deep breath, her rich tones captivating the audience. 'Tonight I am going to share with you the story of my daughter's hamster and my parents' dog and I must warn you that I can't guarantee that no animals were harmed during the making of this tale.'

'You've brought me to a place that tells pet snuff tales? Shame on you,' Hope whispered and a gleam of amusement flickered on Gael's face.

'Compared to some of the stories I've heard here this is practically fluffy and warm.'

'I bet that's what the dog said.' But Hope's mind was whirling. He'd come here before? More than once. Did he sit here and listen, just as he'd sat to the side and taken photos when he was younger? Or did he join in? What did he have to confess? She couldn't imagine him telling a funny story.

'Have you done this?' she whispered as the first audience participant stumbled up onto the stage, pale and visibly nervous as he launched into a tale of wreaking revenge at a school reunion on the bullies who had made his school life a misery. Gael leaned in, his mouth so close to her ear she could feel the warmth of his breath on her bare shoulder. Hope shivered.

'I can't tell you that, I'm afraid. You heard her. What's said in the Hall of Truth stays in the Hall of Truth.' He leaned back and the spot on her shoulder tingled, heat spreading down to the pit of her stomach. Hope drew in a shuddering breath, glancing sideways at Gael. He was concentrating on the stage, his eyes shuttered. Why did he come here to hear strangers speak? And more importantly why had he brought her?

Hope wouldn't have thought it possible that so many people would be prepared to stand up and bare their souls to a room of strangers but, as the first hour ticked by, there was no shortage of willing volunteers. There was a pattern, she noticed. Most ascended the steps nervously, even the ones with confident grins showed telltale signs, the way they tugged at their hands or pulled at their hem. But they all, even the woman who confessed to crashing her husband's car and blaming it on their teenage son, bribing him to take the fall, descended the steps with an air of a weight having been removed from their shoulders, a burden lessened. It was an appealing thought.

The red wine was heavier than she cared for and yet the first glass was finished before she noticed and replaced with a second, which also disappeared all too easily. Gael motioned the waitress over to get their glasses topped up again and a wild idea seized Hope. Maybe she too could lessen some of her burdens. True, she didn't deserve to. But she'd been carrying the guilt around for nine long, long years. Would it hurt to share it? To let this crowd of strangers be her judge and jury.

Her breath caught in her throat, the very thought of speaking the words she'd buried for so long out loud almost choking her. But as the man on stage finished relating a very funny tale of neighbourhood rivalry taken to extremes her mind was made up and when the waitress came over in response to Gael's gesture Hope handed her the slip, slumping back in her chair as the waitress nodded.

What have I done? Her chest was tighter than ever, nausea swirling in her stomach as her throat swelled— her whole body conspiring to make sure she didn't say anything. She glanced at Gael and saw his eyes were fixed on her. Was that approval she saw in their blue-grey depths? He'd brought her here for this, she realised. Wanted her to expose herself emotionally before she did so physically. He was probably right—posing would be a doddle after this.

If she went through with it.

She barely took in the next speaker, her hands clammy and her breath shallow. She swigged the wine as carelessly as if it had been water, needing Dutch courage in the absence of actual courage. She didn't have to do this; she could get up and walk away. She *should* get up and walk away. What was stopping her? After all, her sister's wedding was almost sorted—and if this was the price she had to pay for her career then maybe she needed to reassess her options.

True, Gael wasn't making her do this. Just as he wasn't making her pose for him and yet somehow she was agreeing to do both. He was her puppet master and she was allowing him to pull her strings.

Her head was buzzing, the noise nearly drowning out every other sound and she barely heard her name called. Just her first name, anonymity guaranteed. *She didn't have to do this*...and yet she was stumbling to her feet and heading towards the steps and somehow walking up them, even in the heels from hell, and heading towards the microphone. She grasped it as if it were the only thing keeping her anchored and took in a deep breath.

The spotlight bathed her in warmth and a golden light and had the added bonus of slightly dazzling her so that she couldn't make out any faces on the floor below, just an indistinguishable dark grey mass. If she closed her ears to the coughing, throat clearing, shuffling and odd whispers she might be alone.

'Hi. I'm Hope.' She took a swig of the water someone had thrust in her hand as she had stepped onto the stage, glad of the lubrication on her dry throat. 'I just want to start by saying that I don't usually wear heels this high so if I stagger or fall it's not because I'm drunk but because I have a really bad sense of balance.' Actually after three glasses of Pinot Noir following a dinner comprising of two Pop-Tarts and a banana she *was* a little buzzed but, confessional or not, she didn't see the need to share *that* with the crowd.

Hope took another long slow breath and surveyed the grey mass of people. It was now or never. 'My parents loved to tell me that they named me Hope because I *gave* them hope. They planned a big family, only things didn't work out that way until, after four years of disappointment and several miscarriages, I was born.

They thought that I was a sign, that I was the beginning of a long line of babies. But I wasn't.' She squeezed her eyes shut for a long moment, remembering the desperation and overwhelming need in their voices when they recounted the story of her name to her.

'My childhood was great in many ways. I was loved, we had a nice house in a nice area of London but I knew, I always knew I wasn't enough. They needed more than me. More children. And so my earliest memories are of my mother crying as she lost another baby. Of tests and hospital appointments and another baby lost. I hated it. I wanted them to stop. No more tears, no more hospitals, no brothers or sisters. Just the three of us but happier. But when I was eight they finally gave me the sister I didn't want. They called her Faith…' was that her voice breaking? '…because they'd always had faith that she would be born. And although they still didn't have the long line of children they had dreamed of, now Faith was here they could stop trying. She was enough. She completed them in a way I hadn't been able to.'

The room was absolutely still. It was like speaking out into a large void. 'Looking back, I know it wasn't that simple. They didn't love her more than they loved me. But back then all I knew was that she wasn't told to run along because Mummy was sad or sick or in hospital, her childhood wasn't spent tiptoeing around grief. She had everything and I… I hated her for it. So I pulled away. Emotionally and physically, spending as much time at friends' houses as I could. I pushed my parents away again and again when all I really wanted was for them to tell me I mattered—but they had no idea how to deal with me and the longer they gave me space, the angrier I got and the wider the chasm became. Once I hit my mid-teens it was almost irreparable.

'I wasn't a very good teen. I drank and stayed out late. I wore clothes I knew they'd hate and got piercings they disapproved of. Hung out with people they thought trouble and went to places they forbade me to go. But I wasn't a fool, I knew my best shot at independence was a good education and I worked hard, my sights set on university in Scotland, a day's travel away. And still they said nothing, even when I left prospectuses for Aberdeen lying around. I thought they didn't care.' She took another sip of water, her throat raw with suppressed tears.

'The summer before I was due to go away they booked a weekend away for my mother's fiftieth birthday and asked me to look after Faith. You have no idea how much I whinged, finally extorting a huge fee for babysitting my own sister. I was supposed to have her from the Friday till the Monday morning but on the Sunday I called them and told them they had to come home because I had plans.'

This was the hard bit. True, she had never told anyone what a brat she'd been, how miserable she'd made her family—and herself—but that was small stuff. This, now, was her crime. Her eternal shame. 'I'd been seeing someone, a boy from school, and his parents had made last-minute plans to spend the Sunday night away. I thought I might be in love with him and I didn't want to go to university a virgin, and this seemed like the perfect opportunity to finally sleep together—in his house, in a bed with total privacy.

'I called my parents and told them they needed to

finish their weekend early. That I would be leaving
the house at four and if they weren't back then Faith
would be on her own. It was their choice, I told them,
they were responsible for her, not me. And I put the
phone down knowing that I had won. I had. Right that
moment they were packing their things, their weekend
ruined by their own daughter.' She swallowed, remembering the exact way she had felt at that moment. 'I
knew even then that I was being unfair, I didn't feel
victory or anticipation, just bitterness. At myself for
being such a selfish idiot—and at them for allowing
me to be. I hadn't left them much time to get home so
I think they were distracted, hurrying. They weren't
speeding and my dad was a really good driver. But
somehow he didn't react in time to the truck that pulled
out right in front of him. It was instant, the police said.
They probably didn't feel a thing. Probably.'

Utter silence.

'I didn't lose my virginity that night but I did become a grown-up. I had deprived my sister of her parents and so I took on that role. I gave up my dreams of
university, gave up any thought of carving out my own
life and dedicated myself to raising my sister.' Hope
couldn't stop the proud smile curving her lips. 'I think
I've done okay. I spoiled her a little but she's a lovely,
warm-hearted, sweet girl. And she loves me. But I've
never told her what I did. And I don't know if I ever
will. Thank you for listening.'

He only had himself to blame. He'd wanted to know
what she was hiding, had wanted her to open up and
now she had.

He should be pleased, Hope had shed a layer of armour, allowed her vulnerability to peek through just as he had planned. It would make her picture all the rawer. So why did he feel manipulative? Voyeuristic in a way he hadn't felt even as a teen taking secret photos to expose his classmates?

Because now he knew it all. He knew why she was still a virgin, why she would put her whole life on hold to plan her sister's wedding, why she put herself last, didn't allow herself the luxury of living. And Gael didn't know whether he wanted to hug her and make it better—or pull her to him and kiss her until all she could do was feel.

The way she looked on that stage was terrifying enough: endless legs, huge eyes, provocative mouth. But the worst part was it wasn't the way she looked that had him all churned up inside. It was what she said. Who she was. He had never met anyone like her before.

For the first time in a long time he wasn't sure he was in control—and hadn't he sworn that he'd never hand over control to a woman, to another human being ever again? Because in the end they always, always let you down.

Hope slid into the seat next to him, shaking slightly as the adrenaline faded away. He remembered the feeling well, the relief, the euphoria, the fear. 'Can we go?' she asked.

'Sure. Let me just pay.'

'Great, I'll wait for you in the lobby.' And just like that she was gone, walking tall and proud even in the heels she could barely balance in. His chest clenched painfully. He'd never met anyone like her before. Brave and determined and doing her best to cover up how lost she actually was. He'd spent so long with society queens obsessed with image, with money, with power that he had forgotten that there were women out there who played by a whole different set of rules.

It didn't take long for him to settle up and join her. Hope was standing absolutely still, lost in a world of her own, her dark eyes fixed on something he couldn't see. Guilt twinged his conscience. 'That was a brave thing you did in there.'

'Was it?' She looked at him pensively. 'I don't know. Letting go would be brave. Telling a room full of strangers? I don't know if that's enough.'

'Who else could you tell?'

'Sometimes I wonder if I should let Faith know the truth. If she should know just what kind of person I really am, not worthy of her love and respect.'

'Punish yourself more, you mean? What would that accomplish? Look at me, Hope.' He took her chin gently in one hand, forcing it up so her eyes met his gaze. They were so sad, filled with a grief and regret he couldn't imagine and all he wanted was to wipe the sadness out of them. 'What matters is what you have done in the last nine years and that makes you more than worthy of her love and respect. Don't make her feel that she wasn't a responsibility you accepted joyfully but a burden that you took on through guilt. Think that she's the reason you've spent the last nine years locked away from any kind of normal life. Honesty isn't always the best policy, Hope.'

'You think I should keep lying?'

'Do you love her?'

'Of course I do!'

'Would you sacrifice everything for her?'

'Yes!'

'Then that's your truth. How you got to this point is just history. Goddammit, Hope, the girl lost one set of parents. Don't threaten the bond she has with you as well.' He knew all too well what it felt like to have that bond tossed aside as if it—and he—had meant nothing. 'Come on, I'll take you home.'

But she didn't move. 'I thought we were going out afterwards. You said you knew the perfect place we could go to after the wedding dinner and we should try it out tonight.'

'Haven't you had enough excitement for one night?' He knew he had. He wanted to get back to his studio and draw until all these inconvenient feelings disappeared. This sense of responsibility, of kinship. This stirring of attraction he was trying his damnedest to ignore. So her legs went on for ever, so a man could get lost in her eyes, so he never quite knew what she would say or do next, one minute opinionated and bossy and the next strikingly vulnerable. So he wanted to make everything that had ever gone wrong in her life better. None of this meant anything. Once he'd painted her all these unwanted thoughts and feeling and desires would disappear, poured into the painting where they belonged.

Irritation flashed in her eyes. 'Don't tell me what I have or haven't had, Gael O'Connor. You may have orchestrated tonight but I've been looking after myself for a long, long time. You promised me that I would loosen up and have some fun—well, right now I'm more tense that I think I've ever been so what I need is for you to keep your word and for you to show me a good time.'

Her words were belligerent but the look in her eyes was anything but. She wanted to forget; he understood that all too well. He weighed up the consequences. He should put her in a cab and go somewhere where he could drink until every word she had said on stage was no longer seared into his brain. But common sense seemed less than desirable, everything seemed less than desirable while she stood there in a dress that barely skimmed her thighs, need radiating from her like a beacon. He swore under his breath. He was a fool—but at least he was aware of it. 'Come on, then, what are you waiting for?'

CHAPTER SEVEN

IT WAS A short walk to their destination but, after a swift assessing look at her feet, Gael flagged down a cab, tipping the driver well in advance to make up for the swift journey. It took less than five minutes before the car pulled up and Hope blinked as she took in their surroundings, unable to keep the surprise off her face as she looked around at the massive hotel they'd been dropped off by. As she turned she could see the bright lights of Times Square flashing brashly just a few metres away. 'Every time you take me somewhere you surprise me,' she said. 'Art museums, funny little theatres and now a hotel?'

'We're not going into the hotel proper,' he assured her and steered her past the darkened windows of the hotel to the bar tucked into the ground floor. 'Just into here.'

'Okay,' but she wasn't convinced as he opened the anonymous-looking door and stood aside to allow her to precede him inside. 'It's just this is a hotel bar and it's not really the kind of thing I think Faith is wanting...' She stopped as abruptly as if her volume had been turned down, her mouth still open as she slowly turned and surveyed the room. It was perfect.

Wood panelled and lit with discreet low lights, the piano bar evoked a long-gone era. Hope half expected to see sharp-suited men propping up the bar, their fedoras pulled low and ravishing molls, all red lipsticks and bobs, on their arms.

The long wooden bar took up most of the back wall, a dazzling array of drinks displayed on the beautifully carved shelves behind. A line of red-leather-topped stools invited weary drinkers to sit down and unload their cares into the ever open ears of the expert bartenders. Gael nodded towards a table, discreetly situated in the corner. 'Cocktail?'

Hope weighed up the consequences. A cocktail on top of all that wine? But the five minutes she had spent on stage had sobered her up more effectively than an ice-cold shower and she needed something to alleviate the buzz in her veins. 'Yes. Please. I don't mind what. I know, I'll try one of the house specialities.'

She took a seat, watching Gael as he ordered their drinks. He fitted in here, sleek and handsome with an edge that was undeniably attractive, probably because it was unknown, slightly dangerous. She looked away quickly, hoping he hadn't caught her staring, as he joined her. 'This place is awesome. It's like the New York I hoped to find but haven't yet, if that makes sense.'

'It's exactly like a film set,' he agreed. 'Piano and all. They'll have a jazz band playing on the night of your sister's wedding…'

'So we can come here after the dinner? Oh, Gael, thank you. What a brilliant idea. Faith is going to be so happy. The only thing is it's not that big and there will be fifteen of us. Can we reserve a table?'

He nodded. 'They don't usually but I should be able to...'

'Pull a few strings? I've noticed that. Hunter was right. You know everyone.'

'That's why he sent you to me.'

'Yes. I could never have done this on my own, thank you.'

'I'm not helping you out of the goodness of my heart,' he reminded her.

'Oh, I know, I owe you a debt.' She did but she couldn't begrudge him that, not now. Hope had seen a lot of weddings recently, mostly vicariously through photos shared on social media, far too cut off from her old social group to merit an invitation. They all varied in location, in expense, but the trend seemed to be for huge, extravagant, glitzy events. This small but very sweet wedding she and Gael were putting together in record time made the rest seem tawdry and cheap. It was, she realised with a jolt, the kind of wedding she would want for herself.

The realisation slammed into her and she gripped the table. Would she ever have the opportunity to do this for herself? She wasn't sure she'd know how to date any more, let alone fall in love—and suddenly it was dawning on her just how much she wanted to. Spending the last three days with another human being, a very male human being, had been eye opening. She wasn't entirely sure she always liked Gael; she certainly wasn't comfortable around him. But he challenged her, pushed her, helped her. Attracted her.

Yes. Attracted. Was that so wrong? She was twenty-seven, single, presumably with working parts. Attraction was normal. Only she was a beginner and she was pretty sure he was at super-advanced level. Far too much to handle for her first real crush in a decade. She should start slow. With a man who wore tweed and liked fossils.

Thank goodness, here was her cocktail and it was time to stop thinking. With relief Hope took an incautious sip, eyes watering as the alcohol hit her throat. 'Strong,' she gasped.

'They're not known for their half measures. How are you?'

'Choking on neat gin?'

He raised an eyebrow and she sighed. 'I feel like I've been for a ten-kilometre run or something. It's exhausting baring your soul to complete strangers.'

'I know.'

It was obvious that he did. Either the alcohol or the knowledge he truly had seen everything she was emboldened her to push deeper. 'What did you say? When you went up? You did go up, didn't you? That's how you know it's what I needed.' It had been, she realised. She'd needed to drain some of the poison from her soul.

Gael didn't answer at first, fingering the rim of his glass as he stared into the distance. Hope watched his capable-looking fingers as they caressed the glass in sure strokes and something sweet and dark clenched low inside her.

'I first went there because I was looking for inspiration. My photos felt stale, uninspired. I had just been asked to shoot a series for *Fabled* about the next generation of Upper East Side, all unimaginatively dressed up as Gatsby and co. There they were, ten years younger than my friends and just as entitled, just as arrogant, nothing had changed. I came to the Truth night looking for hope. I didn't expect to be getting up on stage and bearing my soul.' His mouth twisted. 'It could have been professional suicide. I know it's supposed to be confidential but if a journalist had heard me confess how much I hated my work they could have destroyed me.'

'Is that what you said?'

'It's not what I meant to say but near the end it hit me. I was miserable. I needed to change, get back to what I'd originally planned to do—paint.'

'So what did you say?'

'I don't know why but I wanted to tell them about the first time I went to Paris, about the effect the whole city had on me. I'd spent days in the Louvre and so when I went to the Musée d'Orsay I was a little punch-drunk.'

'I can relate to that after this afternoon.'

He grinned. 'Not so punch-drunk that I mixed up Renoir and Degas.' Hope pulled a face at him, absurdly pleased when he laughed. 'Then I saw her, Olympia. I don't know why she struck me the way she did. It wasn't that I found the painting particularly sexy or shocking or anything. But her honesty hit me. I didn't know that relationships could be that honest.'

Hope set her drink down and stared. 'But isn't she a courtesan?'

He nodded. 'And she's upfront about it. There's no coyness, no pretence. "Here I am," she says. "Take me or leave me but if you take there's a price." Everyone knows where they stand, no hard feelings.'

Hope tried to put his words into a context she understood. 'But a relationship, a real one, a lasting one, that's based on honesty, surely.'

'Is that what you believe?'

Was it? She was doubting herself now. 'It's what I'd like to believe.' That much she knew.

'Exactly! You've been sold the fairy tale and you want to believe it's true, but you and me, we live in the real world, we know how rare true honesty is.'

'Hey, don't drag me into your cynical gang of two! What happened to make you so anti love?'

He smiled at that, slow and serious and dangerously sweet. 'Oh, I believe in love. First love, love at first sight, passion, need. I just don't believe in happy-ever-after. Or that love has anything to do with marriage. The marriages I see are based on something entirely different.'

'What's that?'

'Power. Either one person holds all the power and the other is happy to concede it—that's how the whole trophy-wife—or husband, in my father's case, it can be equal opportunity—business works. One half pays, the other obeys. Once they stop being obedient, or they live past their shelf life, then they get replaced.'

'In your crazy world of wife bonuses and prenups maybe, not in the real world.'

'In every world. It may not be as obvious or understood but it's there.'

'But if that was the case then all marriages would fail eventually,' she objected. 'And they don't. Some, sure. But not all.'

Gael shrugged. 'Some people are happy with the imbalance. Or they have equal power and can balance each other out, but that's rare. Now my dad, he keeps marrying women with money. In the beginning they like that he's younger, they think he's handsome, it gives him status—he holds the power. But once they are used to his looks and the lust dies down and they realise their friends aren't so much jealous as amused by their marriage then the power shifts. That's where he is right now. Again.'

'Does he love them? The women he marries?'

'He loves the lifestyle. He loves that they don't demand anything from him. My mom, she held the power because he was absolutely besotted. He tried everything to make her happy. That's her trick. Only in her case she always stays on top. She leaves them when a better deal comes along. Although she's been with Tony for ten years and they have two kids so who knows? Maybe this one she'll stick out.'

'Not all marriages are like that. Your parents were so young when they married.'

'Like Hunter and Faith?'

'Yes.' She wanted to say things would be different for them but how could she when they were still such strangers? But her sister's marriage was hers, to succeed and fail as it would. Hope would help where she could but in this her sister, for the first time in her life, was on her own. 'But they are hardly typical either. Look, you have spent your whole life watching these absurdly rich, absurdly spoilt people play at marriage, play at love, grabbing what they want and walking away the second it gets tough. The real world isn't like that. My parents survived seven miscarriages— seven—IVF. Me,' she finished sadly. She was all too aware just what a strain her behaviour had been on her parents. She would give anything to go back and do it all over again. Yes to Saturday night pizza and films, yes to Sunday walks in the country, yes to that damn carousel ride.

She tried again. 'Look, I might have little real-time experience of love or relationships. I've obviously never been married. But I know something about living up to expectations. If you go around believing everyone is looking to shaft everyone else then that's what you'll find. I don't believe that. I won't.'

His eyes narrowed. 'Look at that, Hope McKenzie all fired up. I like it.'

And she was. She was on fire, living, completely in the moment for the first time in nine years. Her chains loosened, her self-hatred relieved. 'In that case,' she said slowly, scarcely believing the words coming out of her mouth, 'I believe we have a painting to start working on.'

Time stilled as Gael studied her, his eyes still narrowed to intense slits, his focus purely on her. Hope made every muscle still, made herself meet that challenging stare as coolly as she could. If they didn't start this now she wasn't sure she'd ever have the guts to go through with it. But right here, right now, she was ready.

He pushed his stool back and stood up in one graceful, almost predatory movement. 'Yes, it's time,' he said and a shiver ran through her at his words. 'Let's get this painting started.'

The scene was set. He'd planned it all out the day he met her and it was the work of seconds to pull the chaise round to exactly the right angle and to set up the spotlights he used for his photographs to simulate the sun. 'Here,' he said, throwing a clean robe over to

her. 'Go and get changed. Can you screw your hair up
into a high knot?'

Hope nodded. She had barely said a word since they
had left the bar, since her unexpected challenge. But
she'd lost that wide-eyed wariness that had both attracted and repelled him. Tonight she was filled with
some other emotion, an anticipation that pulled him
in. She was ready, ripe for the unveiling.

Gael swallowed. She wasn't the only one full of anticipation. His hands weren't quite steady as he threw a
white sheet over the chaise, adding a huge pillow and a
rumpled flowery shawl. The other models had brought
in their own jewellery, pillows, throws to lie on, things
that had significance to them, but he was painting Hope
in almost identical colours and attitude to the original.
The virgin posing as the courtesan.

'Wait, take this as well.' He handed her a bag.

Hope took it, opening it and peering at its contents.
A thick gold bracelet, a pair of pearl earrings and a
black ribbon to tie around her neck. Mule slippers.
An orchid for her hair. 'Okay. What about make-up?'

'You don't need any. You have perfect skin.'

A blush crept up her cheeks at his words and she
threw him a quick smile before heading off to the small
bathroom he had directed her to just three days ago.
Was that all it was? He'd lost count but what he did
know was that it felt like weeks, months since he had
met her and he didn't want to analyse why that might
be.

It didn't take him too long to set up his tools: paints,
palette, brushes, linseed oil, rags. They evoked a fire
deep inside that his camera and lenses never could;
the messy, unpredictable elements appealed even as

he tried to impose order on his emotions. Gael ran a hand through his hair as he took stock one last time. The setting was perfect, all he needed was his model.

'Hi.' She appeared at the door as if summoned by his thoughts, the white robe clasped tightly around her waist, the mule slippers on her feet. She'd fastened her hair up as directed, the orchid set above one ear, the vibrant pink contrasting with the paleness of her face. Two pearls dangled from her lobes.

'Hi.'

'So where do you want me?' She grimaced. 'Stupid question.'

She walked over to the chaise, slow, small steps, obviously steeling herself as she neared the middle of the room. She halted as she reached the chaise and looked at him enquiringly. 'Do I just…?'

Gael nodded. 'You can drop your robe behind the chaise or hand it to me, whichever.'

'I don't expect it makes much difference. I'm going to end up the same way whichever I do.' But she didn't loosen the robe although her hands were knotted around the tie.

'I could put on some music? If that helps?'

'I don't think so, thank you. Not tonight anyway. Do you need silence while you work or could we talk?'

'I don't mind either way unless I'm focussing on your face. Your mouth will want to stay in one position then but that won't be for a few days.' He usually left conversation up to the models. Some liked to chat away, almost as if they were in a therapy session, others preferred silence, lost in a world of their own. Gael didn't care as long as he got the pose and expression he needed.

Hope walked around the chaise and stared down at the sheet, the pillow, the rumpled shawl. 'Looks comfy.'

'Okay, you've seen the painting. You're propped up on the pillow, your head slightly raised and looking directly at me. One leg casually over the other with the slipper half on, half off—but I can adjust that for you. The arm nearest me bent and relaxed, the other resting on your thigh.' Although she would be fully nude the pose preserved a little bit of modesty, a nod to the Renaissance nudes that had inspired the original pose.

'Got it.' With a visible—and audible—intake of breath Hope untied the robe and slipped it off, handing it to him as she did so. Gael turned away to place it on the floor behind him, deliberately not looking as she lay on the chaise and positioned herself. He had done this exact thing nineteen times before and not once had he had this dizzy sensation, as if the world were falling apart and rearranging itself right here in front of him. Not once had he been both so eager and so reticent to turn around and examine his model.

It's just another model, another painting. But he knew this girl, knew her secrets and her hopes. Had coaxed them out of her so that he could capture her in oils and hang her up, exposed, for all the world to see. Only right now he didn't want the world to see, he wanted to keep this unveiling for himself, her secrets to himself. It was his turn to take a deep breath, to push the troubling, unwelcome thoughts out of his mind and turn, the most professional expression he could muster on his face.

She was magnificent. Almost perfect, as pale as the original except for her legs, tanned to a warm golden brown. Petite and curvy with surprising large breasts proudly jutting out and the sexy curve of her small belly. Every woman Gael had dated boasted prominent ribs and a concave stomach; they looked fantastic in the skimpy designer clothes they favoured but felt insubstantial, as if the real joys in life eluded them. Not surprising when they considered dressing on a salad a treat and cheese the invention of the devil.

She was almost perfect, in a way he hadn't even considered, conditioned as he was by the gym-going gazelles he had been surrounded by for the last fifteen years. Her only flaw was the silver scars crisscrossing the very top of her thighs. There were more lines than he could count, covering the whole thigh from the side round to the fleshy inner thigh. They stopped just where a pair of shorts would end. Where the dress she was wearing tonight had ended, hidden from the world.

She stiffened as his gaze lingered there and when he looked back into her eyes all he could see was shame mingled with hurt pride and something that might be a plea for understanding. 'It hurt when my parents died. It hurt giving up my dreams. It hurt how much I blamed myself. Sometimes it hurt so much I couldn't stand it.'

'You don't have to explain anything to me.' He picked up the yellow ochre and squeezed an amount onto his palette before adding in some cadmium red light, the titanium white close at hand ready to lighten the blend to the exact shade of Hope's upper half.

'Every time I swore it was the last but then the pressure would get too much and the only thing that let it out was blood. For that second, when the blade sliced, I had peace. But then the blood would start to well up and I would feel sick again, hated myself, knew I was so weak. Faith used to ask why I wore old-fashioned swimsuits, you know, with skirts and I pretended it was because I liked the vintage look. In reality I couldn't bear for anyone to see my thighs.' She stopped. 'They will though, won't they? They'll see them on this.'

'I can't exclude them. It would be like editing you. Not quite real.'

'I knew that's what you'd say.'

'When did you stop?'

'When I'd accepted the situation. When it became my reality and not this horrible nightmare with no escape. When I put my old self and my old dreams away and devoted myself to Faith. Then I could cope.'

'Or you exchanged one mechanism for another? How long have you been locked in that box, Hope? How long have you suppressed who you are, what you want, what you need?' His voice had deepened and he wasn't even pretending to mix colours any more, the palette lying in his lap, the brush held casually in his hand as his eyes bore into hers.

'I don't any more. I'm at peace with who I've become.' *Liar*, a little voice inside her whispered.

'That teen rebel who kept a clear head on her shoulders while she did just what she wanted? The girl who had her future planned out down to where she wanted to study and when she was going to sleep with her boyfriend. The girl with dreams which took her away from the family home, away from London. Has she really gone?' His words sent an ache reverberating through her for the lost dreams and hopes she barely even acknowledged any more.

'I am away from London.'

'Still anchored to your family home. To your sister. Still doing the sensible thing.'

'This isn't that sensible,' she whispered.

His eyes pinned her to the pillow; she couldn't have moved if she'd wanted to. 'No.'

Hope had a sense she was playing with fire and yet she couldn't, wouldn't retreat. 'I'm bored of being sensible. So very, very bored.'

'Your hand,' he said hoarsely. 'I just need to position it.'

Hope's mouth was so dry she couldn't speak, couldn't do more than nod in agreement as Gael put the palette down and walked towards her. He had changed into old, battered, paint-splattered jeans and a white, equally disreputable shirt, buttons undone at the neck. She could see the movement of his muscles, a smattering of hair at the vee of the low neck and something primal clenched low down inside her.

She had never been so aware of her own body before, not as a teenager, her mouth glued to her boyfriend's as she fended off his hands, not as she'd stood in the bathroom, razor blade in hand. Every nerve was pulsing, jumping to the increasingly rapid beat of her heart. She could sense Gael over the ever shortening distance, sense him physically as if she were connected to him on some astral plane.

'This hand.' His voice was now so hoarse it was almost a rasp. 'I need it here.'

The second he touched her she gasped, unable to bear the pressure building up so slowly inside her any longer. His fingers on hers, the coolness against the heat of her skin, the sight of those deep olive tones on her own pale hand, the gentle strength inherent in his touch as he moved her. It was as if she had been craving his touch without even knowing it and that one movement opened up a deep hunger inside her.

But she had no doubt, no hesitation. She might be inexperienced but she instinctively knew what to do. She half closed her eyes, watching him through her lashes. 'Here?' She slid her hand a little way along her thigh and, with feminine satisfaction, watched him swallow. 'Or here?' She slid it slightly further so the tips of her fingers met his and, almost of their own volition, caressed the roughened tips.

'Hope...' She didn't know if he was uttering a warning, an entreaty or both but she was past caring. The last few days this man had laid her bare, exposed her deepest secrets and made her confront them. She was tired of confronting, tired of hiding, she just wanted to feel something good—and if her nerves were tingling like this from the mere touch of hand on hand then she had the suspicion this could get really good really soon.

'I think here, don't you?' Her fingers travelled up his hand to explore the delicate skin at his wrist. Gael closed his eyes and Hope thrilled at the knowledge that one simple touch could have such a potent effect, only to draw in a breath of her own as he captured her hand in his, his thumb sliding down to return the favour. One digit, one tiny area of skin but her whole body was lit up like Piccadilly Circus and she knew she couldn't, wouldn't walk away.

She should feel shame or embarrassment lying here wearing nothing but a flower in her hair, a ribbon round her neck while he was still dressed but she didn't feel either of those things. She felt powerful as she tugged at his hand, powerful as in answer to her command he sat at the side of the chaise, powerful as she raised her hand to his face and allowed herself the luxury of learning the sharp cheekbones, the dimple by the side of his mouth, the exquisitely cut lips.

'Hope,' he said again, capturing her hand once again, this time holding it still while he looked deep into her eyes. She saw concern and chafed at it. She saw need and fire and thrilled to it. 'This isn't right. It's been an emotional evening. I can't take advantage of you...'

'Right now I feel like I'm taking advantage of you.'

A primal fire flashed in his eyes and her whole body liquefied as his mouth pulled into a wolfish grin. 'You believe that if you want, sweetheart.'

'Would you be pulling back if I was any other woman?'

'I wouldn't be here if you were any other woman.' The admission was low, as if it had been dragged from him.

Oh.

'That's not what I meant and you know it. If I wasn't a virgin, if you knew I'd been swinging from the chandeliers with a whole regiment of lovers, then would you be pulling away?'

'No,' he admitted. 'But you are and the first time, Hope, it should be special. With someone you love. I don't do love, I don't do long term and I don't want to hurt you. You deserve better.'

'How very teen drama of you. I'm twenty-seven, Gael. I don't know how to flirt or date or *be* in that way. The way things are going I'll be a thirty-eight-year-old virgin and you holding my hand will be the single most erotic thing that's ever happened to me and it would be most unfair of you to condemn me to that. I'm not holding out for a knight on a white charger, you know that. If things were different I'd have lost it to Tom Featherstone nine years ago, in his parents' bed with a White Musk candle to create the mood and James Blunt on the speakers telling me how beautiful I was. I liked Tom. I liked him a lot. I wanted to sleep with him, but I didn't love him and I promise not to fall in love with you. I know you think you're good but you can't be *that* good.'

His mouth curved into a reluctant smile. 'That sounds like fighting talk.'

'It was supposed to be seductive talk.'

The virgin seducing the playboy. It was completely the wrong way round but it turned out that this playboy had scruples. Hope respected them, she just wanted him to get over them already and respect *her* choice.

Gael studied her for a second longer and Hope stared back more brazenly than she ever had, allowing all her need and want and desire to spill out until, with a smothered groan, he leant in, arms either side of her head, his face close to her, mouth within kissing distance, almost.

Hope moistened her lips.

'Let's get this straight,' he said. 'If there's going to be any seducing tonight then I'll be the one who's doing it.'

Her body liquefied again, every bone melting so she felt as if she could simply slide off the chaise to lie in a puddle on the floor—and he wasn't even touching her.

Only then he was, one hand tilting her chin up before he claimed her mouth with his and the last coherent thought Hope knew was that when it came to seduction Gael was right: he was definitely the one in control.

CHAPTER EIGHT

IT WAS ALMOST like a relationship. Almost. The door-man let her straight up without even buzzing first, she had a bag with hot bagels and two coffees in one hand and a Bloomingdale's bag in the other, her toothbrush and a change of underwear in the handbag slung over her shoulder, just in case.

But it wasn't a relationship. When the lift doors opened and she walked into the studio Gael looked up and smiled—which was an improvement on his old non-greeting—but he made no move to come over and kiss her. They didn't kiss, or hold hands, or feed each other titbits or cuddle. They had sex. Every night for the last week and a couple of times in the day as well—after all, she was spending most of the day naked—but they weren't affectionate.

It was as if life was in two halves: the normal half filled with wedding planning, painting, archive sorting and anything else that needed doing—and the secret half. The half when Gael's eyes darkened to a steely blue and just the look in them made her stomach swirl and her pulse speed up. And the two halves were to-tally disconnected.

That very first night, afterwards, he had asked if

she was okay. Probably still worried that she was going to transfer twenty-seven years of singledom into one giant, all-encompassing *'thank you for the first orgasm I didn't sort out on my own'*, wholly inappropriate crush. Obviously all the serotonin and oxytocin had been a little overwhelming; she'd wanted to be completely absorbed in and by and round him while her heartbeat returned to its normal pace and her breathing slowed. Hope completely understood, for the first time, how knee-weakening, chest-tightening, dry-mouthed lust could be mistaken for love.

But she'd spent the last nine years ignoring her wants and wasn't going to let a little bit of—okay, a lot of—sex change the carefully ingrained habits. A wide-eyed, 'So that's what all the fuss is about,' followed by, 'I can't believe it's taken me so long,' wrapped up with a 'thank you' was all that she allowed before wrapping the handy robe around herself and disappearing into the bathroom.

And so she'd reassured him—and herself—that she was more than okay, that she understood exactly what this was. Temporary, fun, no strings, no expectations. Hope guessed that this was what was meant by friends with benefits. Not that they were exactly friends either. Soon to be kind of in-laws with benefits?

Gael threw a pointed look at the industrial clock on the wall. 'Got lost? I thought you were heading back to yours for a change of clothes. Last time I looked your apartment was a ten-minute walk from here.'

Hope felt a slight twinge of guilt. She *was* supposed to be cataloguing again this morning. 'I know I took longer than expected, but I did bring coffee and bagels because, honestly, it is far quicker to go and buy coffee than it is to work that fiendish machine of yours.'

'Coffee from Bloomingdale's?' He nodded at the huge bag in her hand.

'Well, no. I just popped in while I was passing…'

'Passing? Your apartment is straight north from here. How were you passing Third Avenue?'

'Okay, I took a little detour. I know we have an appointment at the bridal shop this afternoon…yes. *We*,' she added firmly as he pulled an all too expressive face. 'I am not going on my own. But Faith needs two gowns and it's stressful enough getting one made up on time, so as the New York dress can be a lot less formal I thought I'd look elsewhere. Besides, I haven't really had a chance to flex the credit card Hunter gave me yet. Shopping with an unlimited budget is a lot more fun than bargain hunting, let me tell you. This might not be an actual wedding dress but it cost more than most entire weddings. I seriously thought they'd added an extra digit by mistake.'

She placed the bag carefully on the floor and opened it. 'What do you think? It was the last in her size so I bought it straight away but now I'm worrying I didn't look at enough options.' She pulled out a delicate cream dress with a lace overlay on the short bodice and cap sleeves, the silk almost sheer around the high waist before cascading into a long pleated skirt. 'I wanted something floaty and unstructured which will be comfortable to wear. After all, she's moving around a lot on the wedding day—Central Park, then to the boat for the afternoon cruise.'

Hope had been unsure what to do with the fifteen guests in the four hours between the cocktails at the

Tavern on the Green and dinner at the Roof Garden. They were such an odd selection of people from Hunter's multimillionaire socialite mother to her aunt and uncle who lived in a small village in Dorset and hated big cities. Luckily inspiration had led her to a small business that chartered boats out and she had booked an old-fashioned sailboat for the afternoon to take the guests on a cruise around Manhattan. It would probably be a little unsophisticated for Misty, who actually owned her own yacht, but Faith and her UK guests would love it.

'Then she's at the Met and finally the piano bar. It's a busy day and she wants white for the party and blessing so I wanted to make sure there was a contrast. It's such a beautiful shimmery cream as well. I got a gorgeous cashmere wrap in a soft gold and both flat shoes and heels so she can swap. What do you think?'

Gael didn't just nod and say, 'Very nice, dear,' as her father used to do. She guessed that was the advantage of wedding planning with an artist and former society photographer. Instead he took the hanger from her and hung the dress from a hook on the wall, standing back, brow creased in concentration.

'Gold accessories?'

Hope felt a little as if she were taking a test. 'Soft gold, not metallic. Because of the thread in the lace.'

'So Hunter and I will need ties in that colour. His dad too probably.'

Hope stared at him, horrified. Suits? She hadn't even thought about suits. Dear God, she wasn't expected to sort the rings out as well, was she?

To her relief Gael carried on. 'My tailor has already started on the suits for the party. A light grey with white linen shirts. You can work with that? We'll order the ties once you have chosen the bridesmaids' dresses. I think we'll want a darker, almost charcoal suit for the wedding, to go with the soft gold accents in the cream of the dress. And a lightweight fabric.' He pulled his phone out and started tapping. How could it be that simple?

Easy, she reminded herself, he had connections. Besides, dress number one had been pretty easy for her thanks to the limitless budget. She'd met up with a personal shopper and this dress was the second she'd seen. She'd fallen for it instantly—more importantly she knew Faith would love it.

Gael looked up from his phone. 'What about you? Have you sorted a dress out yet?'

'No, not yet but I still have a few days. Besides, I don't have a limitless budget so an hour with a personal shopper isn't going to cut it for me. I thought I'd head downtown tomorrow and see what I can find in a soft gold. It's Faith's day anyway so as long as I complement her in the photos it's all good.'

'Hope, just use Hunter's card. He'll be expecting you to use it.' He threw her a shrewd glance. 'But sure, hide away in the background as usual.'

'I'm not! It's her wedding. Some sister I would be if I tried to overshadow her.' Besides, that huge canvas right there? She was in the foreground there. Enough in the foreground to last her a lifetime. 'I'll find something, I promise. Besides, Hunter wants me to put the bridesmaids' dresses for the party on the limitless card so this afternoon I'll spend big. You won't recognise me, my dress will be so attention seeking.'

'I'd know you anywhere,' he said softly and her heart trembled. *No*, she scolded herself. *No reading*

*meanings into words. No thinking this is more than it
is. You escaped awkward if sweet fumblings with Tom
Featherstone for toe-curling, out-of-body-type sex.
How many people go straight to advanced levels, huh?
It's just your emotions are still stuck on beginner level.
Give them a chance to catch up.*

Besides. She wasn't that stupid. She trusted Gael
with her body but there was no way she would trust
him with her heart. She was pretty sure he couldn't
handle his own, let alone somebody else's. No, she
would enjoy this for what it was and when it was over
take the confidence and belief she was gaining day by
day and go out and make herself a happy life. One day
she might even feel that she deserved to.

'We're due at the shop in four hours. Do you need
me to pose?' Airily said but each time she still needed
to take a deep breath before she let the robe slip. Habits of a lifetime were hard to escape and after years of
keeping in the background being under such intense
scrutiny was hard. More than hard.

'No, there's not really enough time. I'm doing some
work on the background so I don't need you. Why don't
you get on with the archive?'

And there she was. Relegated from lover to muse to
wedding planner to assistant in four easy steps. *Know
your place*, she told herself sternly as Gael snagged
the brown bag to take out his coffee—black, two
shots—and bagel—pumpkin seed with cream cheese
and smoked salmon. Both a stern contrast to her own
more adventurous orders but she was a tourist, it was
her duty to experiment. She grabbed her own food
and headed off into the kitchen where her workstation
was set up. She enjoyed the work but this time away

from the office was making her face some uncomfortable truths. She'd hoped this job swap, working with Brenda, would give her the time she needed to work on her career—but instead it was becoming increasingly clear that although she was good at office work and ran events smoothly and meticulously she was bored. In fact she had been bored for a long time if she was honest with herself—something was missing and she couldn't put her finger on exactly what that was.

Hope had fallen into a rhythm over the last week. Gael kept good records and she was beginning to recognise many of the faces so she barely had to put any aside for future clarification. She had already worked her way through his junior year at school and made a good start on senior. The photos were all taken anonymously up to this point but there was a step change the second he was outed: less candid, more posed, less scandalous.

And more of Gael himself. Set-up group shots, time delays. He didn't look at ease, didn't pose, a faraway look on his face as if he was dreaming of being safely back behind the camera.

It wasn't just Gael who made more of an appearance. Time after time the camera lingered lovingly on a willowy blonde girl. She had possibly the most photogenic face Hope had ever seen, the sharp angles and exaggerated features made for the lens. It wasn't just the camera who loved her, judging by the close-ups. The photographer had too.

Hope checked the face against the records she was building up. The girl had been in the junior year pictures as well, only in the background, watching the main players as yearningly as the camera. At some point, like Gael, she had come out of the shadows to shine on centre stage. Tamara Larson.

With half an eye on Gael through the open door, Hope brought up her internet browser and typed in the name. In less than a second it presented her with thousands of possibilities. She pressed randomly on one link. She almost knew what she'd see before the picture loaded: Gael looking down at Tamara, almost unrecognisable. It wasn't just that he was more than a decade younger, slim to the point of skinny, still wearing the gangliness of a very young man. It was the softness in his face, the light in his eyes, the warmth in his smile that made him so alien. Hope had never seen him look that way, not even in their most intimate, unguarded moments.

'I believe in love,' he had said. The proof was right here. He had loved. Adored.

Hope's breath caught in her throat and her fingers curled into fists. It wasn't that she was *jealous*—well, she conceded, maybe just a teensy weensy bit in a totally irrational way but no, in the main it wasn't jealousy consuming her, it was curiosity. Something had happened to wipe that softness out so complexly replacing it with cynicism. What was it?

She clicked back and scrolled onwards until a headline caught her eye. '*Expose* photographer and muse to wed' it screamed in bold type over a picture of a beaming Tamara Larson showing a gigantic—and tacky, Hope sniffed—ring, Gael standing proudly behind her, his hands possessively on her shoulders.

Engaged! He must have still been a baby, younger even than Hunter.

What had happened? There was definitely no so-

cialite living here in the loft. Of course Gael had no
obligation to tell her if he was divorced, none at all.

Hurt flickered inside her. Small but scalding. He
knew everything about her from the scars on her thighs
to the scars on her heart and yet he had shared nothing
that wasn't already public knowledge. No, this definitely wasn't anything like a relationship. For him she
was a convenience; a convenient model, a convenient
assistant, a convenient lover.

Which was *absolutely* no problem. She just needed
to remember, remember exactly what this was—and
exactly what it wasn't.

'Researching?' How had she not heard him come
into the kitchen? Hope jumped guiltily. 'How very
keen.'

'I didn't know you were engaged.' There was no
point in prevaricating; she'd been caught red-handed.

His mouth twisted. 'Briefly. It was a long time ago.'

'What happened?' She saw the shutters come down
and pressed on. 'You're going to have to tell me at some
point. She's going to feature heavily in the retrospective; half your pictures from that time are of her.'

'Tale as old as time: boy meets girl, girl sees opportunity, boy falls for girl, it ends tragically. The end.'
The mocking tone was back but this time it was entirely self-directed. That was worse in some ways than
when he employed it against her.

She tried for a smile, wanting to lighten the suddenly sombre mood. 'Fairy tales have darkened since
my day.'

'Oh, this is no fairy tale. It's an old-fashioned moral-
ity tale of lust, hubris and greed.' He hooked a stool out
and sat down opposite her, leaning on the steel counter-

top, eyes burning with sardonic amusement. 'They rarely have a happy ending.'

Hope was right. He couldn't have a retrospective and not include his own secrets and shame. What would be the point in that? Besides, Tamara was no secret. Their relationship was well documented as the long list of web links on the laptop attested.

Gael spun the laptop round and stared at the photo. All he felt, all he wanted to feel was pity for the poor fool. Standing there looking as if he had won life's lottery, as if the right honeyed words from the right girl were all he needed to count in this world. 'It's really no big deal. It wouldn't be worth a footnote in the retrospective if I hadn't been stupid enough to think I was old enough to get married.'

'But you did get engaged?'

'Does it count as an engagement if the blushing bride-to-be had no intention of going through with the wedding?' He didn't wait for an answer. 'It's not that exciting, Hope. No big romance. Tamara was in the year behind me at school. She was…' he paused, searching for the right word '…she was ambitious. She felt that she belonged at the very top of the social strata; she was beautiful, smart, athletic, rich—but our school was full of beautiful and smart rich girls and somehow she couldn't even get into the inner circle, let alone rule it. She was left out on the fringes.'

'Like you.'

Like him but so much more ambitious. 'Like me. But I knew my place and had no desire to move upwards. I think she knew who I was before I was outed. Sometimes I think she was the one who outed me, because a couple of months before it happened, a few months into my senior year, she started to make a very subtle and clever play for me. Of course I, sap that I was, had no idea. I thought it was the other way round and couldn't believe that this gorgeous girl would ever consider a commoner like me. But the more I noticed her—and she made sure I did—the more I photographed her, the more she made it into *Expose* and the more she featured on the blog the higher her status grew.'

'She might not have planned it. You make her sound like Machiavelli.'

Proof Hope didn't belong on the Upper East Side; the boys and girls he'd gone to school with had studied Machiavelli at preschool. 'Oh, she planned it. She played me like a pro—like father, like son. Suckers for a poor little rich girl every time. No one can make you feel as special as a society goddess, like Aphrodite seducing a mere mortal. We started dating spring break that year and right through my first year at college. I asked her to marry me when she graduated from high school. Can you even imagine?' He couldn't. He couldn't begin to imagine that kind of wild-eyed optimism any more. You'd think his own parents would have taught him just how foolish marrying the first person you fell for was. Turned out it was a lesson he needed to learn for himself.

'She said yes?'

He nodded. 'Oh, she wasn't finished with me yet, and such a youthful engagement ensured she was in the headlines, just where she wanted to be. She dropped out of college to play at being a fashion intern, did some modelling and dumped me for the heir to a hotel empire. I don't think she has any regrets. Her penthouse apartment, properties in Aspen, Bermuda, Paris and the Hamptons more than make up for any lingering feelings she may have had.' He ran into Tamara every now and then. She usually tried to give him some kind of limpid look, an attempt at a connection. He always ignored her.

'You were much better off finding out what she was like before you got married.'

'That's what Misty said. She sent me to Paris for my sophomore year as a consolation prize and that's when I really fell in love.'

'With Olympia?'

He smiled then. 'Olympia and all her sisters.'

'You're lucky.'

'Lucky? Interesting interpretation of the word. Foolish, I would have said.'

'Not for Tamara, for Misty. To have someone who cares. Okay, you lost out a little in the parent lottery. They were too young, too self-absorbed to know how to raise you.'

'Were?' Neither of them had ever grown up, at least where he was concerned.

'But it sounds to me like Misty has always been there for you. Not everyone has that.'

Interesting interpretation. But there was a kernel of truth there that niggled at him uncomfortably. He'd never asked why Misty had kept him after she divorced his father; he'd been more focussed on the fact both biological parents had walked away rather than appreciating the non-biological one who'd stayed. But she *had* kept him. Supported him, still expected him to come and stay every Christmas, Thanksgiving, every summer. She'd have bought him the studio, made him an allowance if he weren't so damned independent. Her words.

He'd always thought that somehow he was fundamentally flawed, unlovable; that was why his parents didn't stay, why Tamara could discard him without a qualm. That was why he only dated women with short-term agendas that matched his, never allowed himself to open up. But maybe he wasn't the one who was flawed after all.

Because it wasn't just Misty who believed in him. He might have bribed Hope into posing, manipulated her into helping him, but she'd responded with an openness that floored him. The painting was almost taking on a life of its own, rawer and more honest than he had thought possible. And then there was the sex…

He'd be lying if he said that was unexpected. There had been a spark between them from the first moment and although he'd been reluctant to take her virginity in the end he'd been powerless when confronted by the desire in her eyes. She was a grown woman and she had made it clear she knew exactly what she was doing.

What was unexpected was how calmly she accepted the situation. No expectations for anything beyond his limited offer. He should be relieved. He wasn't sure what it meant that he wasn't. He was very sure that he didn't want to know.

CHAPTER NINE

LUCKY. SEVERAL HOURS later Hope's words were still reverberating around Gael's head. He'd been called lucky before—when his father married Misty and he stopped being one of 'us', a local, and became one of 'them', the privileged summer visitors. Lucky when he started seeing Tamara, lucky as his career progressed. It had been said with envy, with laughter, with amusement but never before with that heart-deep wistfulness.

He'd never been able to think about that time with anything but regret and humiliation. Tamara's manipulation had been the final confirmation of everything he had suspected since the day his mother had walked out, her next lover already lined up. His subsequent relationships hadn't done much to change his mind, a series of models, socialites and actresses whose beautiful eyes were all solely focussed on what he, his camera and his influence could do for them. The only thing in their favour was that they knew the score, were only interested in the superficial and the temporary and made no demands on his heart or future.

Of course he had never dated outside that narrow world. Never searched for or wanted anything more meaningful. Why would he when so many easy opportunities presented themselves with such monotonous regularity?

Until Hope. She broke the mould, that was for sure. The first woman he had met who seemed to want nothing for herself—he didn't know whether he admired her or wanted to shake her and shout at her to be more selfish, dammit. To *live*. It would be so easy to take advantage of her, to hurt her. Every day he told himself that they should end their affair. And yet here they still were.

Maybe he wasn't the one with the power here after all; in his own way he was as bad as she was, living safely, ensuring his emotions were never stirred, that he remained safe.

Gael scowled, pushing the unwanted thought out of his mind. He *was* challenging himself, opening himself up to potential ridicule with his change of direction. In a few weeks his paintings would be exhibited at one of the most influential galleries in town, exposing his heart and soul in a way that his photos never had. Besides, look at him now. Wedding planning, ordering suits, playing happy families so that his pain of a little brother could have the perfect wedding.

Little brother? He was usually so quick to disassociate himself from any close relationship with Hunter by a judicious 'ex' and 'step'. Just as he always added the 'half' qualifier onto his mother's two children.

Gael shifted, uncomfortable on the overstuffed velvet seat. A few phone calls had led Hope and he here to the exclusive bridal salon popularised on the TV show *Upper East Side Bride*. Women from all over the States—and further afield—travelled here, prepared to pay exorbitant prices for their one-of-a-kind designs, hoping for a sprinkle of rarefied fairy dust to cast a sparkle over their big day.

'I have your sister's measurements and her choices from our available stock,' the terrifyingly elegant saleswoman had said, eyeing Hope as if she were a prize heifer. 'You're a couple of inches too short and a little larger around the bust but I think it's best if you try on the dresses I have selected. That way you'll know how they feel, how your sister will feel when she puts it on.'

Hope had gaped at her, looking even more terrified than when Gael had first asked her to model. 'Me?' she had spluttered but had been whisked away before she could formulate a complete sentence. That had been half an hour ago and Gael had been left in splendid isolation with nothing to occupy him except several copies of *Bridal World* and a glass of sparkling water.

Tamara had never tried on a wedding dress. They hadn't even discussed the guest list. In fact, looking back, she'd shown no interest in anything but the ring— the largest he could ill afford and one she hadn't offered to return.

'Don't laugh.' Hope's fierce whisper brought him back to the here and now. Finally. He'd begun to wonder if this was some form of purgatory where he would be left to ponder every wrong move he had ever made.

Hope teetered into the large room, swaying as if it was hard to get her balance. The private showroom was brightly lit by several sparkling chandeliers and a whole host of high and low lights, each reflecting off the gold gilt and mirrors in a headache-inducing, dazzling display. The walls were mirrored floor to ceiling so he couldn't escape his scowling reflection whichever way he turned. The whole room was decorated in soft golds and ivory from the carpet to the gilt edging on every piece of furniture. A low podium stood before him, awaiting its bride.

Or in this case a bridesmaid masquerading as the bride. A pink-faced, swaying bridesmaid.

'Because Faith's two inches taller they've made me wear five-inch heels,' she complained as she gingerly stepped onto the podium. 'I'm a size bigger as well but they have these clever expanding things so hopefully we'll get an idea but bear in mind that Faith won't spill out the way I am.'

Of course he was going to stare at her cleavage the second she said that—he was only flesh and blood after all—and she was looking rather magnificent if not very bridal, creamy flesh rising above the low neckline of the gown.

The huge, ornate, sparkling gown. It looked more like a little girl's idea of a wedding gown than something a grown woman would wear.

But what did he know? Gael understood colour, he understood texture, he understood structure. Thanks to the work he had done for many fashion magazines he knew if an outfit worked or not. But in this world he was helpless. The second they'd sat down he'd been ambushed with a dizzying array of words: lace, silk, organza, sweetheart necklines, trails, mermaids—mermaids? Really? People got married in the sea?—ball gowns, A-line, princess, crystals. This was beyond anything he knew or understood or wanted to understand, more akin to some fantasy French court of opulent exaggeration than the real world. Marriage as an elaborate white masquerade.

'Say something!'

Hope looked most unbridal, hands on hips and a scowl on her face as she glared at him.

'It's...' It wasn't often that Gael was at a loss for words but he instinctively knew that he had to tread very carefully here. His actual opinion didn't matter; he had to gauge exactly what his response should be. What if this was Faith's dream dress—or, worse, Hope's? He swallowed. Surely not Hope's. Her body language was more like a child forced into her best dress for church than that of a woman in the perfect dress, shoulders slumped and a definite pout on her face.

Gael blinked, trying to focus on the dress rather than the wearer, taking in every detail. There were just so *many* details. A neckline he privately considered more bordello than bridal? Check. Enough crystals to gladden the heart of a rhinestone cowgirl? Check. Flounces? Oh, yes. A definite check. Tiers upon tiers of them spilling out from her knees. It seemed an odd place for flounces to spill from but what did Gael know?

'It doesn't look that comfortable.' That was an under-exaggeration if ever he'd made one; skintight from the strapless and low bust, it clung unforgivingly all the way down her torso until it reached her knees, where it flowed out like a tulle waterfall. If Gael had to design a torture garment it would probably resemble this.

'It's not comfortable.' She was almost growling. 'Worse, I look hideous.'

'You could never look hideous.' But she didn't look like Hope, all trussed up, tucked in and glittering.

Hope pulled a face. 'Now you start complimenting me? Don't worry, Gael, I don't need your flattery.'

Was that what she thought? 'I don't do flattery. But

if you want honesty then I have to say that dress doesn't suit you. But you're not looking for you and I don't know your sister at all.'

She studied herself in the mirror. 'She did short-list it but I don't think she'd like it. I can't imagine her picking it in a million years but who knows? Even the sanest of women, women who think a clean jumper constitutes dressing up, get carried away when it comes to wedding dresses. This was designed for a reason. Someone somewhere must think it's worth more than a car. But no, I don't think Faith would. Still, it's not up to us. Take a photo and email it to her.'

The next dress was no better unless Faith dreamed of dressing up as Cinderella on steroids. The bead-encrusted heart-shaped bodice wasn't too bad by itself—if copious amounts of crystals were your thing—but it was entirely dwarfed by the massive skirt, which exploded out from Hope's waist like a massive marshmallow. A massive marshmallow covered in glitter. Gael didn't even have to speak a word—the expression on his face must have said it all because Hope took one look at his open mouth and raised eyebrows and retreated, muttering words he was pretty sure no nicely brought-up Cinderella should know.

He very much approved of dress number three. Very much so, not that it was at all suitable unless Faith was planning a private party for two. Cream silk slithered provocatively over Hope's curves, flattering, reveal-ing, promising. Oh, yes. He approved. So much so he wanted to tear it right off her, which probably wasn't the response a bride was looking for. Regretfully he shook his head. 'Buy it anyway, I'll paint you in it...' he murmured and watched her eyes heat up at the promise in his voice as she backed out of the room.

'I like this but I think it's too simple. She's already wearing one flowy dress, I think she wants something a bit more showy for the party.'

Gael looked up, not sure his eyes could take much more tulle or dazzle, only to blink as Hope shyly stepped onto the podium. 'I like that,' he said—or at least he tried to say. His voice seemed to have dried up along with his throat.

He coughed, taking a sip of water as he tried to re-gather himself. Brought to his knees—metaphorically anyway—by a wedding dress? Get a grip. Although Hope did look seriously...well, not hot. That wasn't the right word, although she was. Nor sexy nor any of the other adjectives he usually applied to women. She looked ethereally beautiful, regal. She looked just like a bride should look from the stars in her dark eyes to the blush on her cheek.

Looked just like a bride should? Where had that thought come from? He'd attended a lot of weddings, many of them his parents', but right up to this moment Gael was pretty sure he'd never had any opinion on how a woman looked on her wedding day. It was this waiting room, infecting him with its gaudiness, its dazzle, its femininity.

But Hope did look gorgeous. The dress was decep-tively simple with wide lace shoulder straps, which showed provocative hints of her creamy shoulders, and a lace bodice, which cupped her breasts demurely. The sweetheart neckline was neither too low nor too high and the skirt fell from the high waist in graceful folds of silk. She was the very model of propriety until she turned and he saw how low the back of the dress swooped, almost to her waist, her back almost fully exposed except for a band of the same lace following the lines of her back.

'I've seen statues of Greek goddesses who look like you in that dress.'

'I look okay, then?' But she knew she did. Look at the soft smile curving her mouth, the way she glowed. Not only did she look incredible, she obviously felt it too.

'Is this the one, then?' An unexpected pang hit him as he asked the question. Not at the thought of the day's purgatory finally ending, but because Hope should buy that dress for herself, not for someone else. It was hers. It couldn't be more hers if it had been designed and made for her. But here she was, ready to give up the perfect dress to her sister, just as she had given up everything for Faith every day for the whole of her adult life.

'I don't know.' Hope was obviously torn. 'I really, really love it. It's utterly perfect. But is it right? She asked for a showstopper for the party and this is too simple, I think. Take a photo and send it but I'm not sure she'll pick it.'

Gael disagreed. His show had been well and truly stopped the second Hope appeared in the dress. 'Whatever that dress is it isn't simple.'

'It *is* the most gorgeous dress I have ever seen. I can't imagine finding anything more beautiful. But I'm not sure it's what Faith has in mind.'

'There is a whole salon of showstopping dresses you haven't tried on yet,' Gael said, heroically reconciling himself to another several hours of dazzling white confections. 'Let's fulfil the brief and get your sister what she wants. But, Hope, you look absolutely spectacular in that dress. You should know that.'

She looked at him, surprise clear on her face. Surprise and a simple pleasure, a joy in the compliment. 'Thank you. I feel it, for once in my life I really do.'

Gael stood back and surveyed the painting before looking over at Hope, lying on the chaise in exactly the same position she had assumed every day for the last eleven days. She had complained that she was so acclimatised to it she was sleeping in the same position now. 'I think we're done.'

'Really done? Finished and done? Can I see?' Gael hadn't allowed her to take as much as a peep at her portrait yet and he knew she was desperate to take a look. 'I need to, to make sure you haven't switched to a Picasso theme and turned me blue and into cubes. Actually, that might be easier to look at. I vote Picasso.'

'No to the blue cubes, possibly to taking a look and no, not finished, but I don't need you for the second pass, that's refinement and detail. I have photos and sketches to help me for that. But I am absolutely finished for now. I'm going to let it dry for a few days and then work on it some more.'

Hope was manoeuvring herself off the couch, as always reaching straight for the white robe, visibly relaxing as she tied it around herself. 'It's good timing. Faith gets here in what, three hours? We've got a fitting almost straight away. Tomorrow I am going to walk her through the whole wedding day and then we have afternoon tea with Misty. I hope Faith's happy with the decisions we made. Not that she has much choice at this late hour.'

'If she isn't then just point out that rather than frolic in Prague she could have sorted it all out herself.'

Hope ignored him. 'Wednesday is the hen do all day—that's a spa day, afternoon tea, Broadway show followed by dinner and cocktails and then Thursday is the actual wedding. Friday we recover while the happy couple love it up in the Waldorf Astoria and then it's the blessing and party on Saturday. So it's a good thing you don't need me. I don't have any time to pose this week. I've just about finished the archiving as well. Brenda has a designer and a copywriter ready to start working with you the second that contract is signed.'

Which meant they were done. He didn't need her to cross-reference any more photos or pose and the wedding was planned. So where did that leave them? Funny how they had been heading to this point for nearly two weeks and yet now they were here he felt totally unprepared.

Because he *was* unprepared. The wedding was the end date; they both knew it. He'd finish his paintings and prepare for his show, she'd go back to DL Media and complete her time here in New York before heading back to London. Yet he felt as if something wasn't finished. As if *they* weren't finished.

Gael swallowed. It had been a long time since he'd cared whether a relationship was over or not. And this wasn't even a relationship, was it?

It wasn't meant to be… His chest tightened. Of course, it most definitely wasn't. He didn't do relationships, remember? Because that way he didn't get hurt. Nobody got hurt. And he'd told her that right from the start.

So why was he feeling suddenly bereft?

Hope kicked off the mule, stretching out her leg. 'Thank goodness that's over with. Do you know how uncomfortable it is holding your leg in that one position for hours at a time? So, may I see?' Hope nodded at the easel and gave Gael her most appealing smile. 'I know nothing about art anyway, so you know my opinion isn't worth anything.'

He narrowed his eyes. 'Why do you do that?'

'Do what?'

'Put yourself down. Your opinion is worth a lot more than most of those so-called critics who will make or break me in three weeks' time. Because it's genuine. Because somewhere hidden deep inside you have heart and passion and life if you'd just let yourself see that. But you never will, will you? Far easier to wallow and self-deprecate and hide than put yourself out there, risk falling or heartbreak again.'

He wanted to recall the words as soon as he'd said them as she physically recoiled, staring at him, her face stricken. 'I put myself out there. Good God, in this last two weeks all I've done is try new things.'

He could apologise. He *should* apologise but he kept going, dimly aware he wasn't so much angry with Hope as he was with himself. Angry because at some point he'd broken his own rules and started caring—and he hadn't even noticed. Angry because yet another person was about to walk away out of his life and not look back—and he had no idea how to stop her. 'You've let me lead you into new things. You followed. That's not quite the same thing.'

She straightened, her colour high and her eyes bright with anger. She looked magnificent. 'Oh, excuse me for not walking in here and stripping off and begging you to paint me. Of course, where I come from that behaviour can get a girl arrested but why should that have stopped me?'

'You never tell me that no, you don't want steak you want Thai, you never say no, I don't want red wine I'd like white even though I *know* you prefer white. You don't tell me what ice cream you prefer so I end up buying out the whole store. You don't tell me when your legs have cramps and the pose hurts. You don't tell your sister that organising a wedding in two weeks is impossible.'

'Because those things don't matter to me. I wanted to help Faith. I genuinely don't care what wine I drink. Why are you saying this?'

Gael stood back from the easel, his eyes fixed on her, expression inscrutable. 'Tell me this, Hope. Tell me what you want to happen next. Tell me what we do tomorrow when you no longer have to come here. What we say to your sister, to Hunter. Tell me how it ends.'

Tell me how it ends. There was no point telling him anything because no matter what he said there was no real choice. It would end. Today, Sunday, when she went back to the UK—only the date was in doubt.

She had to focus on that because if she thought about everything else he had said she would collapse. Was that how he saw her? She always thought of herself as so strong, as doing what was needed no matter what the personal cost. But Gael didn't see a strong woman. He saw a coward.

I know you prefer white.

She did. Why hadn't she said so? Because she was so used to putting other people's needs, their feelings first at some point it had become second nature. Well, no more.

'It has ended. It ended when you put that paintbrush down. We no longer have anything to offer each other.'

'So that's what you want,' he said softly.

Yes! No! All she knew was that it wasn't a choice because if he could make her feel like this, this lost, this hurt, this needy, after less than two weeks then she had to walk away with her heart and pride intact. Or at least her pride because it felt as if something in her heart were cracking open right now. It shouldn't be possible. She knew who he was and what he was and she had kept her guard up the whole time and yet, without even trying, he had slipped through her shields.

Without even trying. How pathetic was she? He didn't need to do anything and she had just fallen in front of him, like her aunt's dog, begging for scraps. The only consolation was that he would never know.

'You knew I preferred white and bought red anyway?'

The look he shot her was such a complicated mixture of affection, humour and contempt she couldn't even begin to unravel it. 'All you had to do was say.'

Affecting a bravado she didn't feel, she walked forward until she was standing next to him then turned and looked at the painting.

It was at once so familiar and yet so foreign. The pose, the setting so similar to the painting she had now seen so many copies of she could probably reproduce it blindfolded—but this was magnified. No dog, no servant, no backdrop, the attention all zoomed in on Hope. Her eyes travelled along her torso, from the so casually positioned slipper along her legs. She winced as she took in the scars, each one traced in silvery detail, an all too public unveiling.

The actual nudity wasn't as bad as she'd feared, not compared to the scars. She was curvier, paler, sexier than she had expected; she looked like a woman, not like the girl she felt inside. Her breasts full and round, even the slight roundness of her stomach suggested a sensual ease.

But her face… Hope swallowed. 'Do I really look that sad?'

Unlike Olympia she wasn't staring out at the viewer with poise and confidence. She wasn't in control of her sensuality. She looked wary, frightened, lost. She looked deeply sad.

Gael was watching her. 'Most of the time, yes. I paint what I see, Hope. I tried to find something else, thought if you confronted some of your sadness I could reach a new emotion but that's all there was.'

All there was. She wasn't just a coward, she was a miserable one.

'Between the scars and my emotions you have exposed everything, haven't you?' Hope whispered.

'I didn't expose anything, Hope, it was all right there.'

But it wasn't, it hadn't been, she'd hidden it all under efficiency, under plans, under busyness, until even she had no idea how she felt any more. It had taken his eye to see it and strip her bare until she couldn't hide any more. 'I hope you're satisfied, Gael. I hope this painting brings you fame and fortune. I hope it's worth it. But at the end of the day that's all you'll have. You tell me I'm a coward? I'm not the one recreating pictures of an idealised woman. I'm not the one cold-shouldering the family who love him, who care for him, who have done nothing but support him even when they no longer had any legal link. I'm too afraid to go for what I want? I'm not the only one. You'd rather photograph life, paint life than live it.'

Hope would have given anything to make a dramatic exit but unless she wanted to walk through the grand marble foyer, past Gael's doorman and out into the streets in a white robe that was never going to happen. She changed as quickly as she could, gathering all her belongings and stuffing them into a bag. It didn't take long. She'd practically lived here for the past eleven days, heading back to her own tiny apartment every couple of days to get a change of clothes, but she had left no residue of herself. Her bag didn't even look full and it was as if she had never stepped foot inside— apart from the painting, that was.

She walked back through the vast studio. At what point had the picture-covered brick walls, the cavernous empty space, the mezzanine bedroom begun to feel like home? Hope took one last look around; nothing would induce her to return.

Gael certainly wasn't going to make the effort. He was leaning by the window, a beer in one hand, looking out at the skyline. He barely turned as she walked by.

'I guess I'll see you at the wedding,' Hope said finally, glad that her voice didn't wobble despite the treacherous tears threatening to break through the wall she was erecting brick by painful brick.

'I guess.'

She pressed the lift button, praying it wouldn't take too long. 'Bye, then.'

He looked up then. 'Hope?'

Her namesake flared up then, bright and foolish.
'Yes?'

'You deserve more. You should go and find it. Believe it.'

She nodded slowly as the flare died down as if it
had never been, leaving only a bitter taste of ashes in
her mouth. 'You're right, Gael. I do deserve better.
See you around.'

CHAPTER TEN

'DO I LOOK OKAY?'

Gael turned to see Hunter pull at his tie, trying to fix it so it was perfectly aligned, pulling at the knot with nervous fingers until it tightened into a small, crumpled heap. Otherwise he looked like a young man on the cusp of a life-changing moment, shoulders broad in the perfectly cut suit, eyes bright and excited and a new maturity in his boyish face.

'Here,' Gael said gruffly, trying to hide the pride in his voice. 'Let me.'

He had taught Hunter how to tie a tie in the first place, how to ride a bike, how to swim. He'd bought him his first beer and listened through his first infatuations. And now his little brother was moving on without him, going forward, past Gael into a whole new life. 'There you go.' He stood back and surveyed him. 'I don't know what Faith sees in you but you'll do.'

Hunter still looked pale but he managed a smile. 'She's wonderful, isn't she? I don't know what I did to deserve her. I'm the luckiest man alive.'

He really believed it too; there was sincerity in every syllable. All credit to Misty for bringing up such a decent young man. Gael had known plenty of men with lesser looks, lesser pedigrees and lesser fortunes who prowled the earth believing themselves young gods. Hunter genuinely didn't believe his face, name or income made him any better than anyone else—it just made him work harder to prove he deserved his privilege. Gael had only met Faith once briefly, two days ago after her afternoon with her new mother-in-law, but had quickly decided that either she was the world's best actress or as genuinely besotted by Hunter as he was with her.

He had hoped to see Hope, to try and make some kind of amends so that the next few days wouldn't be too awkward, but Hope hadn't been with her sister. He hadn't seen her since she'd walked away without a backwards glance. Not since he'd allowed her to. It was better for them to be apart; they both knew it. So why that bitter twist of disappointment when Faith had announced that her sister had gone shopping—and why this even more twisty and unwelcome anticipation as he savoured the knowledge that in just an hour's time she would be by his side?

They were both adults. They had spent two enjoyable weeks together. She had inspired him to create one of the best paintings he had ever done, even if it wasn't exactly what he'd set out to paint; he was thinking of calling it Atlas—because she looked as if she were carrying all the cares in the world on her slim shoulders. They could meet to celebrate this wedding as friends, surely? But when he thought of her in that wedding dress, glowing, when he thought of her lying on the chaise, posed and perfect, when he thought of her in his bed, then 'as friends' seemed a cold and meagre ambition.

But what was the alternative? Ask her out properly? They had said everything that needed to be said; he knew her more intimately than some men knew their wives of fifty years. How could he go from that to the kind of dating he did? The kind of dating he was capable of? Premieres, dinners in places to be seen, superficial and short-lived. He couldn't but he knew no other way.

He didn't *want* to know any other way. Because his way couldn't go wrong. It ended without tears, without acrimony, without devastation. It was safe. There was nothing safe about Hope and the way he was with her—harsh, unyielding, pushy. He wanted too much from her and she let him demand it. But, oh, how he liked it when he surprised her; her face when he had laid out all the different tubs of ice cream. Like a small child set loose in a toy store. She almost made him believe he could be the kind of man who lived a different way. Almost.

He pushed the thought away. Today wasn't about him and, despite his attempts to deny kinship, he was proud that Hunter had asked him to stand by his side. 'You ready?'

Hunter nodded. 'I was ready the first day,' he said simply. 'I saw her walking towards me and I just knew.'

Gael's mind instantly flashed back to the moment he had first seen Hope. What had he known? Surprise that she wasn't the woman he was expecting, yes. Annoyance at the delay in his plans? Absolutely. Recognition? He would like to deny it but something had made him keep her there, manipulate the situation so she stayed with him. He didn't want to dwell too much on what his reasons might have been. He attempted humour instead. 'Knew she was hot?'

'Knew she was the one for me. I was prepared to learn Czech or German or French, whatever I had to do to talk to the girl with eyes like stars—you can imagine my relief when I discovered she was English! Not that it would have made any difference whatever nationality she was. We would have found a way to communicate.'

'Hunter, you've known her what, two months? And it's not like your mom has had the best track record with the whole happy-ever-after thing. Are you sure you're not rushing into things?'

'Man, I am totally rushing into marrying Faith. Full pelt. I just know that she's the one for me and I'm the one for her and I can't wait to get started on our adventures together. As for Mom? She'd be the first to say she never listened to her heart. She didn't trust it not to lead her astray so she married strategically, for fun, for friendship—and then ended up divorced anyway.'

When had Hunter got so wise? Gael straightened his own tie, unable to look the younger man in the eye. 'I don't know what a good marriage is. What makes a relationship worth fighting for.' The confession felt wrought out of him and he turned slightly so that Hunter wouldn't be able to see his expression.

'I think it's when you trust someone completely and their happiness means more to you than your own—and when you know that they feel exactly the same way. You balance each other out, make the other person safe.'

Balance. What had he said to Hope? That marriage was about power? Hunter was saying the same thing only he saw it as a positive thing. That allowing someone else the power just made you stronger. Gael was almost light-headed as he tried to work it out. But looking at Hunter, so happy and so *confident*, he couldn't help but wonder if he possessed a knowledge Gael just couldn't—or wouldn't—understand.

He didn't have much time to dwell on his stepbrother's words as the next hour was a flurry of activity, first meeting up with Hunter's father and the two friends the groom had invited to this small, intimate celebration, and then they had to make their way to Central Park and the little lakeside glade where Hunter and Faith would be making their vows. Hunter didn't seem at all nervous, laughing and joking with his friends and patiently listening to all his father's last-minute advice—and who knew? Maybe Hunter's father did know what he was talking about because not only had he stayed good friends with Misty but he had clocked up fifteen years with his current wife, a record amongst all the parental figures in Hunter's and Gael's lives.

In no time at all they were at the lake, which had been made ready according to Hope's detailed instructions; a few chairs had been arranged in a semicircle either side of the little rustic shelter under which Hunter and Faith would make their vows. White flowers were entwined in the shelter and yellow and white rose petals were scattered on the floor. All against Central Park's stringent regulations but the Carlyle name had persuaded the officials that an exception could be made.

Gael looked up at the cloudless sky and smiled; somehow Hope had even persuaded the weather to comply and the rain and wind which sometimes heralded the beginning of September had stayed away. Hunter's father and friends took their places while Gael

stood beside his brother at the entrance to the pavil-
ion, making polite conversation with the official who
was conducting the short service. But what he said
he hardly knew. In just a few minutes he would see
her—and the spell her absence had cast would be broken. She'd walked away before he had decided it was
time. That was all this sense something was amiss
was. Nothing more.

He turned as he heard feminine voices, his heart
giving a sudden lurch, but it wasn't Hope, merely a
group of hot-looking women dressed in bright, formal
clothes, fanning themselves and giggling as they took
their seats. They were accompanied by one harried-
looking elderly gentleman who breathed a sigh of relief as he took in the other men. Hope's uncle must
have felt fairly overwhelmed by all the womenfolk he
had spent the last three days escorting around the city.

He took a brief headcount as Misty wafted in,
looking as elegant and cool as ever. The five men in
Hunter's party, Misty, the bride's uncle and aunt and
four young women who must be her two cousins and
two friends. They were all here except for the bride
herself—and her bridesmaid. He took a deep breath
and steeled himself. It had been a brief fling, that
was all. He bumped into old flames all the time and
didn't usually turn a hair. There should be nothing
different this time.

Shouldn't be and yet there was.

And then the string quartet, placed just out of sight
around the curve in the path, struck up and the small
congregation rose to their feet and turned as one. Every
mouth smiled, every eye widened, many dampening
as Faith floated towards them in the ethereal designer

dress Hope had chosen for her beloved sister. Her hair was twisted into loose knots with curls falling onto her shoulders, she carried a small posy of yellow and white roses and her eyes were fixed adoringly on her groom. But Gael barely took any of it in, all his attention on the shorter woman by her side. Faith had asked her sister, the person who had raised her, to walk her down the aisle both today and for the blessing in two days' time.

Gael was the only person there who knew how much this gesture cost Hope. How touched she was but also how full of grief that their father wasn't there to do it—and that she would be symbolically relinquishing the last of her immediate family to someone else. That the moment she stepped back she truly would be alone.

His chest swelled with empathic grief because although her full mouth was curved in a proud smile and her carriage straight her eyes were full of tears and the hand holding a matching posy was shaking slightly.

Hope's hair was also tied up in a loose knot with a cream ribbon looped around, contrasting with the darkness of the silky tresses. She wore a knee-length twenties-style dress in a slightly darker shade than her sister's soft golden cream; she was utterly beautiful, utterly desirable. Damn. That wasn't the reaction he had been hoping for at all.

Hope looked up as if she could feel the weight of his gaze. Her lips quivered before her eyelashes fell again. *Look at me*, Gael urged her silently. *Let me work out what's happening here.* But his silent plea fell flat and although she smiled around at the gathered audience she didn't look at him directly again, not once.

* * *

The day was at once eternal and yet it passed in a flash. One moment Hope was kissing her sister's cheek, knowing that this was the last time she would be her next of kin, her first confidante, her rock, the next she was listening as Hunter promised to take care of Faith for ever.

She believed him. They were absurdly young but there was a determination and clearness amidst the starry-eyed infatuation that made her think that maybe they had a shot at making it work. Faith had grown up so much it was impossible to take in that the sisters had only been apart for three and a half months.

They moved seamlessly from ceremony to drinks, from drinks to the boat, which dreamily sailed around Manhattan in a gentle ripple of sparkling waters and blue skies before the cars took them to the now shut Met for a VIP tour followed by dinner. Now, at the end of the day, they were back at the speakeasy, reserved exclusively for the wedding party until midnight; there had been a last-minute panic when Hope realised that Faith's age meant she would be unable to enter the premises if it was open to the public. The bar didn't usually do private parties but a quiet word from Gael had ensured their cooperation; she wouldn't have been able to organise half of the day without him. He knew exactly who to speak to, how to get the kind of favours Hope McKenzie from Stoke Newington wouldn't have had a cat in hell's chance of landing. She should say thank you.

She should say *something*. They had been in the same small group of people for ten hours and somehow avoided exchanging even one word. She should tell him that he was wrong about her, that when it mattered she would always stand up for herself; she should tell him that, uncomfortable as his painting made her, she still recognised what a privilege it was to be immortalised that way. She should thank him for all his help with the wedding. She should tell him that two weeks with him had changed her life.

But she didn't know where to begin. She was just so aware of him. They could blindfold her and she would still reach unerringly for him. She knew how he tasted, she knew how his skin felt against hers. She knew what it felt like to have every iota of his concentration focussed on her. How did people do it? Carry this intimate knowledge of another human being around with them? She hadn't expected this bond, not without love.

Because of course she didn't love him. That would be foolish and Hope McKenzie didn't do foolishness. She wasn't like her sister; she couldn't just entrust her heart and happiness to somebody else. Especially somebody who didn't want either and wouldn't know what to do with them even if he did.

The sound of a spoon tapping on a glass recalled her thoughts to the here and now and, as the room hushed, she looked up to see Faith balancing precariously on a chair, her cheeks flushed.

'Attention,' her sister called as the group clapped and whistled. 'Bride speaking.'

Hope slid her glance over to Gael and, as she met his eyes, quickly looked away, her chest constricting with the burden of just that brief contact.

'I know we're doing speeches on Saturday,' Faith said when she had managed to quieten the room. 'So you'll be glad to hear this isn't a speech. Not a long one anyway. I just wanted to say thank you to my big sister.'

Hope started as everyone turned their attention from Faith to her. She shifted awkwardly from foot to foot, cursing her sister as she met the many smiles with a forced one of her own. Faith knew how much she hated attention.

'There are so many thank-yous I owe her that I could keep you here all night and not finish. Most of you know that Hope raised me after our parents died. You might not know that she gave up her place at university to do it, that she planned to study archaeology and travel the world, instead she became a PA and worried about bills and balanced meals and cooking cakes for the PTA bake sale. She refused to touch the money our parents left us, raising me on her salary— and I never did without. It was only recently that I realised that while *I* didn't go without, Hope often did. But she never made me feel like a burden. She always made me feel loved and secure and like I could be or do anything.' Faith's voice broke as she finished that sentence and Hope felt an answering lump in her own throat, a telltale heat burning in her eyes.

She heard a gulp of a sob from her aunt and a murmur from Misty but her eyes were fixed on her sister. The two of them against the world one last time.

'She gave me this amazing day, the best wedding day a girl could have asked for, with only two weeks' notice. She has always, always put me first. Now it's time she put herself first and I am so happy that she's decided to quit her job and go travelling.'

'What?' Hope wasn't sure if anyone else heard Gael's muffled exclamation as the room erupted into applause. 'I know she can afford to do it by herself but, Hope, I hope you will accept this from Hunter and me.' Faith held out an envelope. 'It's a round-the-world ticket and an account with a concierge who will organise all the visas and accommodation you need. It doesn't even begin to pay you back for all you've done and all you are but I just want you to know how much I love you—and when Hunter and I start a family I just hope I can be half the mother you were to me.' Faith was clambering off the chair as she spoke and the next minute the two girls were in each other's arms, tears mingling as they held each other as if they would never let each other go. Only Hope knew as she kissed her sister's hair that this was them letting go, this was where they truly moved on.

'Thank you,' she said as she reluctantly and finally moved back. 'You absolutely didn't have to...'

'I wanted to. So did Hunter. It gives you three months to explore the US and South America before taking you to Australia, then New Zealand and from there to Japan and across Asia. You choose when and where—as long as you turn up in Sydney in three months' time because that's when we'll be there and I hope you'll join us for that leg.'

'You can count on it.' She knew this was the right thing for her to do, to start living some of the dreams she'd relinquished all those years ago. The world might seem larger, scarier—lonelier—than it had back then, but she was a big girl now. She'd cope. But as she glanced over at Gael's profile a sense of something missing, something precious and lost shivered through her. She couldn't leave without making sure things were mended between them. It wouldn't be the same, not after the things they had said, but she wasn't sure she would have had the courage to move on without him. He should know that. Because she knew he was broken too.

CHAPTER ELEVEN

IT WAS NEARLY MIDNIGHT. A car was waiting outside to whisk Hunter and Faith back to the Waldorf Astoria where they had a luxury suite booked for two nights. Hope would see Faith in less than forty-eight hours at the blessing and party in Long Island but as she hugged her new brother-in-law and kissed her sister goodbye it was as if she was saying goodbye to a whole portion of her life.

The bride and groom departed in a flurry of kisses and congratulations and the party began to disperse as the bar staff efficiently began to set the room back up ready to reopen to the public. Hope's aunt and uncle were taking their daughters and Faith's friends back to the apartment Hope had booked for them, a day of non-wedding-related sightseeing waiting for them the next day. Hope had excused herself from joining them with the excuse that she still had some arrangements to finish for the Saturday—but in reality all she wanted to do was lie in her apartment and work out the rest of her life. She fingered the envelope her sister had given her. She had a year's hiatus at least.

'Congratulations on the travel plans. It seems a little sudden though.' She shivered as Gael came up beside her, not touching and yet so close she could feel every line of his body as if they were joined by an invisible thread. Her body ached for him; she wanted to step back and lean into him and let him absorb her. Typical, first time she tried for a light-hearted fling and she was having to go full cold turkey, knowing one touch would drag her back in.

Okay, deep breath and light chit-chat. She could do this. 'Sudden or really overdue. I was always going to go travelling after university. I had my route planned out. Lots and lots of ruins. Machu Picchu, the Bandelier national monument, Angkor Wat...' Her voice trailed off as she imagined setting foot in the ancient places she had dreamed about studying.

'What about Brenda, the job you wanted so much?'

'I phoned her yesterday and handed in my notice. I know it seems that I'm just jumping into it but I'm not. It turns out there's plenty of time to think at a spa day. I lay there on a massage table covered in God knows what, baking like a Christmas turkey, and your words echoed round and round.'

He caught her wrist and pulled her round to face him. The nerves in her wrist jumped to attention, shooting excited signals up her arm.

'I was out of line.'

'You were right,' she said flatly. 'I let life happen to me—I only did the job swap because Kit told me to apply. If he hadn't I would still be in Stoke Newington, missing Faith, wearing baggy tunics with my hair four inches too long because regular haircuts feel like an extravagance, getting the same bus to work, eating the same sandwich on the same bench every lunchtime and not even allowing myself to dream of anything better. Thinking I didn't deserve anything better.'

They moved aside with a muttered apology as a waiter pulled another table into place and a waitress pulled chairs across the floor, their legs screeching as they dragged on the wood. Gael winced. 'Let's get out of here. We're going the same way, at least let's share a cab.'

A cab pulled up almost the second they hit the pavement and Gael opened the door. 'Will you come back to mine?' he asked as she climbed in. 'I have a bottle of white in the fridge. I would really like to clear the air before the party. We're almost related now, after all.'

He'd bought a bottle of white wine. It was too little too late but it was something. 'Okay.' They did need to clear the air. The last thing she wanted was for Faith to know that they had been involved; it was all too messy.

They didn't speak again until they reached his studio. It was only three days since she had last walked through the lobby, greeted the night porter and taken the exclusive lift that led up to Gael's penthouse studio but she felt as if she had been away for months, suddenly unsure of her place in this world.

'Wine?' Gael asked as they stepped into the studio and Hope nodded. He'd bought it for her after all, a peace offering, it would be rude to say no.

She kicked off the pretty, vintage-style Mary Jane shoes, uttering a sigh of relief as her feet were freed from the straps and three-inch heels. She looked around, unsure where to sit. The chaise held too many memories, there was no way she was heading up the winding staircase to the small mezzanine, which contained a bed and very little else—and there was no other furniture in the place. Hope placed her shoes on the floor and followed Gael through to the kitchen instead, perching herself on one of the high stools as he poured wine from a bottle with an obscure—and expensive-looking—label.

'To new adventures,' she said, taking the glass he slid over to her and raising it in a toast. 'My travels, your exhibition.'

'When are you off? A month's time?'

Hope took a sip of the wine. Oh, yes. Definitely expensive. You wouldn't get a bottle of this in a price promotion in her local corner shop. 'No. Next week.'

'Next week?' He set his glass down with an audible clink. 'Didn't you have to work out your notice?'

'No, thanks to you signing the contract I was so far in Brenda's good books that she's offered me a year's sabbatical. I don't know if I'll take it. Who knows what I'll want to do or where I'll want to be in a year's time but there is a job with DL Media if I need it, which is reassuring.' She grimaced. 'It's not easy being spontaneous all at once. Baby steps.'

'But next week! Don't you have to plan and pack and sort out an itinerary?'

Hope pulled the envelope Faith had given her out of her bag. 'No, thanks to Faith. These people will sort it all out. I tell them where I want to go and they make sure I do. They're already looking at converting my work visa here to a tourist one and sorting out everything I need for South America. I'll spend a couple of days shipping some things home and sorting out what I need and then I'll be ready to go. It's working out really well actually. Maddison is coming to New York to clear the rest of her things out of the studio. If I leave she can cancel her rent. I don't think she's planning on coming back to the city.'

It would be interesting to meet her life-swap partner, the woman who captured Kit Buchanan's heart. Funny how a six-month change of locations could alter things irrevocably. Maddison was engaged, moving countries, her whole world changing. Hope might be more alone than ever but at least she was no longer staying still.

'You have it all organised, as always.' There was a bleak tone in Gael's voice she didn't recognise but when she glanced at him his expression was bland.

'The plane ticket is first class as well. I can't believe they did this.'

'I can. Your sister loves you, Hope.'

'For the first time in nine years I feel unburdened. Free. I'll always miss my parents and I'll always regret the person I was but I'm ready to forgive myself.' She forced herself to hold his steady, steely gaze. 'Thanks to you, Gael. I'll always be grateful.'

'You won't be here for the opening night of the exhibition.'

'No.' She blinked, surprised at the sudden change of subject. 'I'm not sure I could have faced it anyway. People looking at me and then at the painting. It'd be a little like the nightmare when I'm walking down the street naked. Only it would be real.'

'That's a shame. I wanted you there.' He paused while Hope gaped at him, floored by the unexpected words. He wanted her at his big night? As a model—or to support him? 'Look. I wanted to let you know that I've decided not to show it, your painting.'

Time seemed to stand still, the blood rushing to her

ears as she tried to take in his words. 'But, you need it. The centrepiece. It's less than three weeks away.'

'I have nineteen pictures I am proud of. Nobody else knows I planned a larger twentieth. I'm not sure that I'll ever paint a better picture than the one I did of you but I don't need to show it. I'd rather not, knowing it makes you so uncomfortable.'

He was willing not to show the picture? After everything he had done to persuade her to pose? Even though he thought it was the best he had done? Hope had no idea how to respond, what to say. This graciousness and understanding was more than she had ever expected from anyone. She slid off the stool and walked to the door, pausing for a second as she took in the easel with the large canvas balanced perfectly on it dominating the empty space and then, with a fortifying breath, she went over to take a second look.

It wasn't such a shock this time. Her skin was as white, her body as nude, she still wished she'd done daily sit-ups so that her stomach was concave rather than curved but, she conceded, her breasts looked rather nice. Biting her lip until she tasted blood, Hope forced herself to step in and examine her scars, remembering the pain and the secrecy and the self-hatred that went into every one of the silvery lines.

She pulled her gaze away from her torso and looked into her own eyes. Sad, wary, lonely. That was who she was; there was no getting away from it, no hiding. She shouldn't blame Gael for painting what he saw. She could only blame herself. Well, no more.

'Show it,' she said. 'I want you to. It's real. Maybe one day you can paint me again and I'll be a different person, a happier one.'

'You can count on it.' He was leaning against the door, watching her, hunger in his eyes. She recognised the hunger because she felt it too. Had felt it all day, this yearning to touch him, for him to touch her. For the world to fall away, to know nothing but him and the way he could make her feel; sexy, adored, power-ful. Wanted.

She was leaving in less than a week. What harm could it do, one last time?

'On Saturday we're the best man and the brides-maid once more. We have busy, sensible roles to play.'

The hunger in his eyes didn't lessen; if anything it intensified. 'I know.'

'Sunday I'm helping Faith get ready to go off on her travels and then I need to spend a couple of days preparing for mine.'

Gael pushed away from the door frame and stalked a couple of steps closer. 'Hope, what are you saying?'

Deep breath. She could do this. 'I'm saying that this is the last time we can be ourselves, Hope and Gael. Painter and model. Carousel riders. Storytellers.' She moistened her lips nervously. 'Lovers.'

'Last time?'

She nodded.

He smiled then, the wolfish smile that sent jolts of heat into every atom in her body, the smile that made her toes curl, her knees tremble and her whole body become one yearning mass. 'Then we better make the most of it, hadn't we?'

The morning sun streamed in through the huge win-dows, bathing the bed in a warm, rosy glow. Gael had barely slept and now he rolled over to watch Hope slumber, the dawn light tinging her skin a light pink, picking out auburn lights in her dark hair.

He felt complete, that all was right in his world. Probably, he decided sleepily, because Hope and he had tidied up their brief relationship, ending it in a mutually agreeable and agreed manner. No more messy arguments or avoiding each other, no more hurt emotions or dramas. Instead a civilised discussion and one last night together before they went their separate ways. Neat, tidy and emotionless. Just how he liked it.

It was a shame she wouldn't be there for the opening night though; he would have liked to have seen her reaction when all the pictures were displayed together for the first time with her at the very heart of the show.

He trailed his finger over her shoulder, enjoying the silky feeling of her skin. She was right. Tomorrow they had their roles to play and those roles didn't involve making out on the dance floor. Probably for the best that they had agreed last night was to be the final time.

But right now, in dawn's early light, was in between times, neither last night nor today. They were out of time, which meant there were no rules if they didn't want there to be. And that meant he could press his lips here, and here, and here…

'Mmm…' Hope rolled over, smiling the sleepy yet sated smile he had come to know and enjoy. 'What time is it?'

'Early, very early, so there's no need to think about getting up yet,' he assured her, dropping a brief kiss onto her full mouth, shifting so his weight was over her. 'Can you think of any way to spend the time as we're awake?'

Her eyes, languorous and sleepy, twinkled up at

him, full of suggestion, but she put her hands onto his chest and firmly, if gently, pushed him off. 'Plenty, but none suitable for people who are just friends.'

'Ah.' That wasn't disappointment stabbing through his chest. He could walk away at any time, after all. 'We've reached the cut-off point, then.'

'I think it might be wise.' She sat up, the sheet modestly wound around her. The message was clear—*I'm no longer yours to look at or touch or kiss*. 'Besides, I could do with an early start. Your stepmother—ex-stepmother—has asked me to go to Long Harbor this evening and stay so that I'm there for the morning when the caterers and everyone arrives. I know this party is all her work but I think she'd appreciate some backup. You'll be with us Saturday before three p.m., won't you? That's when my family arrives, with the blessing ceremony due to start at four.'

They were back in wedding-planning mode, it seemed. Gael slumped back onto the pillows, curiously deflated. 'I'll be there.'

'Great. I'll see you then.' Hope slid off the bed, still wrapped in a sheet, and headed towards the stairs. She turned, curiously dignified despite her mussed-up hair, her bare feet, the sheet held up modestly, just her shoulders peeking out above its white folds. 'Thank you, Gael. For waking me up, for challenging me, for making me challenge myself. I'm not saying I'm exactly relaxed about giving up my job—even with a sabbatical as a safety net—and if I think too hard about travelling by myself I get palpitations here.' She pressed her hand to her stomach. 'But I know it's all really positive—and I don't think I would have got here on my own. So thank you.'

'You'd have got there,' he said softly. 'You just needed a push, that was all. You were ready to fly.' He wanted to say more but what could he say? He didn't have the words, didn't have the feelings—didn't allow himself to have the feelings—so he just lay there as she turned with one last smile and watched her walk down the stairs. And five minutes later, when he heard the elevator ping and knew that this time she really had walked out of his studio for the last time, he still hadn't moved. All he knew was that the complete feeling seemed to have disappeared, leaving him hollow.

Hollow, empty and with the sense that he might have just made the biggest mistake of his entire life.

Five hours later the feelings had intensified. Nothing pulled him out of his stupor, not working on the painting—that just made the feelings worse—not going over his speech for the next day, not proofing the catalogue for his show. The only thing that helped was keeping busy—but he couldn't keep his mind on anything. Finally, exasperated with the situation, with himself, Gael flung himself out of the apartment, deciding if he couldn't work off this strange mood he would have to run it off instead. He stuck his headphones on, selected the loudest, most guitar-filled music he could find and set off with no route in mind.

Almost inevitably his run took him through Central Park, past the carousel and down towards the lake. Every step, every thud of his heart, every beat an insistent reminder that last time he was here, the time before that and the time before that he wasn't alone.

Funny, he had never minded being alone before. Preferred it. Today was the first day for a long time that he felt incomplete.

It didn't help that everywhere he looked the park was full of couples; holding hands, kissing, really kissing in a way that was pretty inappropriate in public, jogging, sunbathing—was that a proposal? Judging by the squeal and the cheering it was. Were there no other single people in the whole of Central Park? With a grunt of annoyance Gael took a path out of the park, preferring to pound the pavements than be a bystander to someone else's love affair.

He. Preferred. Being. Alone. He repeated the words over and over as his feet took him away from the park and into the residential streets of the Upper East Side. The midday sun was burning down and the humidity levels high but he welcomed the discomfort. If you were okay on your own then no one could ever hurt you. If he hadn't loved his mother so much then her absence wouldn't have poisoned every day of his childhood. If he hadn't relied on his father so much then it wouldn't have been such a body blow when his father left him behind with Misty. If he hadn't fallen so hard for Tamara then her betrayal wouldn't have been so soul-guttingly humiliating.

You could only rely on yourself. He knew that all too well.

And yet he couldn't shake Hope's words. *You're lucky to have Misty, to have someone who cares.* Hunter had wanted—no, needed—him by his side yesterday. Misty hadn't just paid his school and college fees, she had given him a home, shielded him from his father's impulsive and destructive post-divorce lifestyle. In those tricky few days after his authorship of *Expose* became public knowledge she had stood by him. She insisted he came to her every Thanksgiving and Christmas even now.

Hope had seen that when he couldn't—or wouldn't. But then she knew all about being a mother figure, didn't she?

And now it was her time to shine. He wished he could see her as she finally visited the places she had always wanted to visit, could capture the look on her face as she finally reached Machu Picchu, in photographs, in pencil sketches, in oils. He could draw her for ever and never run out of things to say about the line of her mouth, the curve of her ear, that delicious hollow in her throat.

His steps slowed as he gulped for air, his discomfort nothing to do with the heat or his punishing pace. Somehow, when he hadn't even noticed it, Hope McKenzie had slid under his guard and he could walk away—leave her to walk away—and it would make no difference. She'd still be there. He'd still be alone but the difference would be now he'd feel it. He'd not just be alone—he'd be lonely.

He bent over, trying to get his breath back and re-order his thoughts, and as he straightened he saw a familiar sign, the shop they had visited so recently, the shop where Faith's wedding dress still hung, the last alterations completed, ready to be steamed and conveyed to Long Island in the morning. The shop where Hope had tried on a dress that, for one moment, had made him wish that he were a different man, that they had a different future. A dress that belonged to her.

Was this a sign or just a coincidence? It almost didn't matter. What mattered was what he chose to do next.

CHAPTER TWELVE

'You look beautiful.'

Hope smoothed down her dress and smiled at Gael, her heart giving a little twist as she did so. By tacit consent they had kept their distance from each other all day except when posing for photographs, but now the evening had drawn in and the event moved from celebration to party the rules they had set themselves didn't seem quite so rigid. They were aiming for friends, after all.

'It's all the dress. Lucky I had some expert help choosing it.' All the bridesmaids wore the same design, a halter-necked knee-length dress with a silk corsage at the neck, but while the other four bridesmaids' dresses were all a deep rose pink Hope, as maid of honour, wore a cream and pink flowered silk. 'If your show is a flop you could always turn your hand to wedding styling. You have quite the knack.'

'All I did was nod in the right places. I think you knew exactly what you were looking for.'

'Maybe. So that was a good speech you did back then.' She'd heard lots of people talking about it—and him. It was hard to keep a bland smile on her face when she kept overhearing beautiful, gazelle-like girls in dresses that cost more than her entire wardrobe discussing just how sexy they thought he was and speculating whether his net worth was high enough for a permanent relationship or whether he was just fling material.

They weren't lying about how sexy Gael looked today. Some men looked stilted or stuffy in a suit; Gael wore his with a casual elegance and a nonchalance that made a girl sit up and take notice. Even this girl. Especially this girl.

His tie was the same dark pink as the flowers on her dress. They looked as if they belonged together.

Funny how deceiving looks could be.

'Thank you. Hunter deserved something heartfelt and not too cruel. He's a good kid. Although now he's a married man I suppose I shouldn't call him a kid.'

'I suppose not.' Hope looked over at the dance floor where her sister swayed in her new husband's arms, the two of them oblivious to the two hundred or so guests Misty had invited. It was a beautiful party. Lanterns and fairy lights were entwined in the trees all around and in the several marquees that circled the dance floor, one acting as a bar, one a food tent, one a seating area and one a family-friendly place with games and a cinema screen for the younger guests.

The swing band that had accompanied the meal had been replaced by a jazz band crooning out soulful ballads as the evening fell. A sought-after wedding singer was due to come onto the purpose-built stage at nine to get the dancing really started and then a celebrated DJ would entertain the crowd into the early hours. The blessing had been beautifully staged and even though

Hope had seen her sister make similar vows just two days before she had still needed to borrow a hanky from her aunt when she welled up for the second time.

'Would you like to dance?'

The question took her by surprise. 'I don't know if that's wise. Maybe later when the music is less...'

'Less what?'

'Less sway-like. I hear the wedding singer does an excellent Beyoncé. I'll dance with you to that.'

'It's a deal.'

So they had made small talk and it wasn't too hard, made civilised plans for later. No one looking over at them would think that they were anything but the best man and the maid of honour relaxing after a long day of duties. Good job on both sides. It was probably time to drift away to opposite sides of the dance floor so Hope could resume sneaking peeks at him while pretending even to herself, especially to herself, that she wasn't.

The night after the wedding had been her gift to herself. A chance to be bold and brave. A way of ensuring that something sweet and special didn't turn sour, that her memories of Gael and her time with him were something to savour. A time for her to take control and show them both just what she could do, who she could be. And then she had walked away with her head held high. Chosen when, chosen how.

So why did her victory feel so hollow? She had a sinking feeling it was because things weren't finished between them, much as she tried to fool herself that they were. There had been a tenderness that night she hadn't felt before. A closeness that she wasn't sure she believed was real and not just a figment of her over-heated imagination. Truth was, Gael knew her better than anyone else in the entire world. How did she walk away from that?

But she didn't know what the alternative was or if she was brave enough to explore it. Hope turned away from the dance floor. Ahead of her, through the small scrub-like trees, was a private path that led directly to the beach. She'd been meaning to take a look at the ocean but hadn't had a chance to. 'I'm going to take a walk,' she said, kicking her shoes off, taking a couple of steps away. She didn't know if it was devilry or the moonlight that made her swivel back around and aim a smile in Gael's direction. 'Coming?'

He didn't answer but his movement was full of intent and she didn't demur as he took her hand, leading her through the trees with sure steps. The path through the trees was lit with tiny storm lanterns swaying in the slight breeze like an enchanted way.

All Hope knew was the salt on her lips, the sea breeze gentling ruffling her elaborately styled hair, the coolness of the sand between her toes and the firmness of Gael's grip. 'What was it like living here?'

He didn't answer until they cleared the trees and reached the top of the dunes. The beach spread out before them, dim in the pearl glow of the moon, behind them Hope could hear music and laughter, ahead the swish of the waves rippling onto shore.

'I didn't feel like I belonged,' he said finally. 'I was a scrubby kid who biked around Long Harbor getting into trouble, the kind of kid begging for a chance to go out on a boat, trying to find ways of earning a few dollars through running errands. Home was chaotic, living with my grandparents, I always fell asleep listening to the music in the bar downstairs. And then I came here. A driver to take me where I needed to go, money, more than I could spend, a boat that belonged to the family I could take out whenever I wanted complete with a crew. And when I fell asleep at night it was to total silence. I had a room, a study and a bath all to myself.'

'How did it feel?'

'Like I didn't know who I was.' His hand strengthened in hers. 'I still don't. Except...'

She wasn't sure she dared ask but did anyway. 'Except what?'

'These last couple of weeks I've had an inkling of who I could be, the kind of man I'd like to be.'

'Me too. Not the man part but the seeing a new way. It's not easy though, is it?'

Letting go of his hand, Hope sank down into the soft sand, not worrying about stains on her dress or if anyone was looking for her or if there were things she should be doing. All those things were undoubtedly true but she didn't have to take ownership of them. Gael folded himself down beside her with that innate grace she admired so much and Hope leaned into him, enjoying his solid strength, the scent of him. The illusion that he was hers.

'You've made a good start though. Travelling, carefree, no plans.'

'Hmm. On the surface maybe,' she conceded. 'I want to go, don't get me wrong, but there's still the little voice in my head telling me I don't deserve it. And another little voice shrieking at me to plan it all down to the final detail, account for every second because if it's planned it can't go wrong.'

'Sounds like it's getting crowded in your head.'

'Just a little. Planning makes me feel safe so trying to learn to be more spur of the moment is, well, it's a challenge. My real worry is...' She hesitated.

'Go on.'

'Being lonely,' she admitted. 'Even lonelier than I have been because I have always had Faith and a job, a routine. I'm not good at talking to people, Gael. I suck at making friends. A whole year of just me for company looms ahead and it terrifies me.'

'Oh, I don't know. It sounds pretty good to me.'

Surprise hit her *oomph* in the chest. In her heart. Not just the words but the way he said them. Low, serious and full of an emotion she couldn't identify. Her pulse began to hammer, the blood rushing in her ears, drowning out the sound of the sea. She'd always wanted to matter to someone, be worthy of someone, but at some point in the last two weeks her goalposts had shifted.

She wanted to matter to Gael.

Proud, cynical Gael. A man who gave no quarter and expected none. A man who knew what he wanted and pushed for it. A man who had made her confront all her secrets and sins and forgive herself.

A man who made her feel safe. Worth something.

'You could travel,' she said, looking down at her feet, at the way her toes squished into the sand. 'Do the whole Gauguin thing.'

'Been reading up on your history of art?'

'I remember some things from my whistle-stop tour.'

'I could. I could travel, stay here, move to Paris or

Florence or Tahiti. I'm not sure it would make much difference though. I'd still be hiding.'

'What from?'

'Myself. From emotion. From living. Do you know why that painting of you is the best thing I have ever done?'

She still couldn't look at him, shaking her head instead.

'Because I felt something when I painted it. Felt something for you. Complicated, messy, unwanted human emotions. Lust, of course. Exasperation because I could see you hiding all that you are, all that you could be. Frustration that you didn't see it. Annoyance because you kept pushing me, asking awkward questions and puncturing the bubble I had built around myself.'

Exasperation, annoyance. Frustration. At least she had made him feel something.

'And I liked you. A lot. I didn't want to. The last thing I needed was a dark-eyed nymph with a wary expression and a to-do list turning my carefully ordered world upside down.'

'Is that what I did?' She raised her head and looked directly at him, floored by the unexpected tenderness in his smile.

'I think you know you did. I have something to show you. Will you come?'

She nodded mutely.

Gael pulled Hope to her feet and led her back along the path to the house, skirting the party and the merry-making guests, neither of them ready or able to make small talk with Hunter's Uncle Maurice or Misty's drunken college room-mate. He took a circuitous route round the Italian garden and in through a side door that only he and Hunter had ever used as it led straight into a boot room perfect for dropping sandy surfboards and towels and swim trunks with a shower room leading right off it. It was empty today, no towels folded on the shelves, no boards hanging on the wall, no crabbing nets leaning in the corner. For the first time Gael felt a shiver of fond nostalgia for those carefree, summer days. He might not have ever admitted it but this huge nineteen-twenties mansion had at some point become his home—just as its mercurial, warm-hearted, extravagant owner had become his mother.

The boot room led into a back hallway, which ran behind the reception and living areas, avoiding the famous two-storey main hallway with its sweeping, curved staircase and ornate plasterwork. Instead Gael led the way up a narrow back stairway, once used solely by the army of servants who had waited on Misty's great-grandparents, the original owners of the mansion.

'I feel like I'm a teenager again, sneaking girls up to my room through the back stairs.'

'Was there a lot of that?'

'No, sadly not. I was too grand for the girls I grew up with and not grand enough for the girls Misty introduced me to. Besides, there wouldn't have been any sneaking. Misty would have offered us wine and condoms and sent us on our way. She was embarrassingly open-minded. Nothing more guaranteed to make a teen boy teetotal and celibate—even if he wasn't a social pariah!'

'I bet there were hundreds of girls just waiting for

you to look in their direction,' Hope said. 'I would have been.'

'Maybe,' he conceded. He had been so filled with his own angst he would never have noticed.

A discreet door led onto the main landing. Closed again, it blended into the wooden panelling. The house was riddled with hidden doors and passageways and he knew every single one of them.

'Don't think I'm not appreciating this behind-the-scenes tour of one of Long Island's finest houses but where are we going?'

'Here,' Gael said and, opening the door to his own suite of rooms, ushered her inside.

It hadn't changed much since he first took possession of the rooms as a boy. A sitting area complete with couch, a TV and a desk for studying. The computer console was long gone and the posters of bikini-clad girls replaced with paintings he admired by local artists, but the window seats still overlooked the beach and the Victorian desk was still piled with his paints and sketchbooks. A door by the window led into his bedroom.

'These are yours?'

'Misty apologised when she assigned them to me, said she hoped I wouldn't be too cramped but she thought I'd prefer not to be stuck out in one of the wings.'

Hope wandered into his bedroom, her eyes widening as she took in the king-size bed, the low couch by the window, and she opened the door to his bathroom complete with walk-in shower and a claw-foot bathtub. 'You poor thing, it must have been such a chore making do with just the two huge rooms and a bathroom fit for an emperor.'

'I managed somehow.'

Now she was here, now the moment was here, unexpected nerves twisted his stomach. What if he had got her, got them, got the situation wrong? For a moment he envied Hunter his certainty. He'd known, he'd said, the second he'd seen Faith. They had been together for just two months and there they were downstairs, husband and wife.

He'd known Hope for less than three weeks but he couldn't imagine knowing anyone any better after three years.

He looked over at her as she stared out of the window at the moon illuminating the sea. Her hair was still twisted up, held with a rose-pink ribbon, the dress exposing the fine lines of her neck and the fragile bones in her shoulders. Desire rippled through him, desire mixed with a protectiveness he had never experienced before, an overwhelming need to protect her from life's arrows. She'd already been pierced too many times. 'I got you something.'

She turned, a shy smile lighting up her face. 'You didn't have to.'

'I know. It's not a parting gift. It's an *I hope you come back* gift.'

Her mouth trembled. 'Really?'

Words failed him then, the speech he'd prepared during the sleepless night. Words telling her he wanted her to go, to experience, to live. But at the end of it all he hoped she'd choose to come back. To him. 'It's in the closet.'

With a puzzled frown wrinkling her forehead, Hope

opened the door to his walk-in closet. It was practically empty, the few essentials he kept here folded up and put away on shelves at the back. There was only one item hanging up.

Hope stood stock-still, one hand flying to cover her mouth. 'My dress.'

'I didn't think anyone else should have it.' It was hers. They had both known it the second she had put it on. Every line, every delicate twist of lace, every fold of silk belonged to her.

'But…it's a wedding dress.'

'I don't want to confine you, Hope. I don't want you to go away tied down. I want you to live and laugh and if you love then that's the way it's supposed to be.' He swallowed as he said the words, alternate words trembling on his tongue. *Stay with me.* 'This dress is a talisman, a pledge. That if you choose to come back to me then I'll be here. And if you don't, well. It's yours anyway. If you want it.'

Did she understand? Did she know what it meant that he had asked her to come back to him? He had never asked anyone before. Never exposed himself. Taken each desertion on the chin and then wrapped another layer of protectiveness around himself.

Hope couldn't take her eyes off the dress, perfect as it hung in the closet, every fold exactly where it should be. It did belong to her, he was right. Nothing had ever felt so right—nothing but being in Gael's arms. And he had bought it for her.

The dress had been exorbitant but she knew it wasn't the dollar price that made it special, utterly unique. It was the gesture behind the gift. It was opening himself up to rejection. It was allowing her the power to reject him. That was his real gift. He was giving her power. He trusted her with his heart just as she had trusted him with her body and soul.

'Come with me,' she said. 'Travelling. You can paint anywhere, can't you? Come with me.'

'But it's your big adventure.'

'And I want to share it with you.' That was what had been holding her back. Her dream travels seemed ash grey when she contemplated doing it alone. She wanted to share each discovery, each experience with Gael. She wanted him to tease her, to push her, to make her feel, to stretch herself. 'I have done since I booked it. I knew I should be excited but instead every time I thought about getting on that plane, flying away from you, I felt sick with dread.'

'You really want me along?'

'Always.' She put her hand on his shoulder and instantly knew she was home, that no matter where she was in the world if he was there she would be settled. 'When Faith told me she was marrying someone she barely knew I thought she was crazy. Well, people will tell me I'm crazy, that two weeks is nothing at all, but I have lived a lifetime in the last fortnight. A lifetime with you. It wasn't always easy or comfortable but for the first time in a long time I was alive. You brought me to life. I didn't think that I knew what love was, that I was capable of it, that I deserved it, but you have made me change my mind. I love you, Gael. I love you and I want to spend the rest of my life having adventures with you.'

His eyes had darkened to a midnight blue as he pulled her in close, caressing her with light scorching kisses along her brow, her cheeks, her mouth. Hope pressed herself as close as she could, her hands holding on tightly as if she would never, ever let go. And she wouldn't; this man was hers. She knew it with every fibre of her being and her body thrilled with ownership. He was hers and she was his.

'I love you,' he said, the words catching in his throat. 'I didn't want to, I fought against it but I think I loved you from the first moment you unleashed your outrage on me.'

'I'd barely said hello and you asked me to strip,' she protested. 'Gael, will you come with me? I don't want to be away from you, from us, but I don't want to walk away from a chance to do something new again. If I don't travel now I never will.'

'On one condition.' He smiled into her eyes. 'Monday you put on that dress and we go to City Hall and get married. I'll need to be in New York in three weeks for the exhibition launch party but otherwise I'm yours for the next year. For the rest of my life. What do you say?'

'I say you'd better ask me properly.'

She was only teasing but Gael stepped back, dropping to one knee, like a picture from a fairy tale. Hope's heart stuttered with longing and love as he took her hand in his. 'You'd better say yes now I'm down here.'

'Ask the question and then I'll be able to answer.'

'Hope McKenzie. Would you do me the honour—the very great honour of being my wife?'

She didn't answer straight away, taking a moment to take in the devilish glint in his eye mingling with the love and tenderness radiating from him. Hope dropped down to kneel in front of him, taking his face in her hands as she did so. 'Yes. Yes, I will. Always.' And as she leant in to kiss him she knew that her adventures were only just beginning and that she would never be lonely again, not while she had Gael by her side.

* * * * *

If you enjoyed this story, make sure you've read
Maddison and Kit's story
IN THE BOSS'S CASTLE
Available now!

MILLS & BOON®
Hardback – September 2016

ROMANCE

To Blackmail a Di Sione	Rachael Thomas
A Ring for Vincenzo's Heir	Jennie Lucas
Demetriou Demands His Child	Kate Hewitt
Trapped by Vialli's Vows	Chantelle Shaw
The Sheikh's Baby Scandal	Carol Marinelli
Defying the Billionaire's Command	Michelle Conder
The Secret Beneath the Veil	Dani Collins
The Mistress That Tamed De Santis	Natalie Anderson
Stepping into the Prince's World	Marion Lennox
Unveiling the Bridesmaid	Jessica Gilmore
The CEO's Surprise Family	Teresa Carpenter
The Billionaire from Her Past	Leah Ashton
A Daddy for Her Daughter	Tina Beckett
Reunited with His Runaway Bride	Robin Gianna
Rescued by Dr Rafe	Annie Claydon
Saved by the Single Dad	Annie Claydon
Sizzling Nights with Dr Off-Limits	Janice Lynn
Seven Nights with Her Ex	Louisa Heaton
The Boss's Baby Arrangement	Catherine Mann
Billionaire Boss, M.D.	Olivia Gates

MILLS & BOON®
Large Print – September 2016

ROMANCE

Morelli's Mistress	Anne Mather
A Tycoon to Be Reckoned With	Julia James
Billionaire Without a Past	Carol Marinelli
The Shock Cassano Baby	Andie Brock
The Most Scandalous Ravensdale	Melanie Milburne
The Sheikh's Last Mistress	Rachael Thomas
Claiming the Royal Innocent	Jennifer Hayward
The Billionaire Who Saw Her Beauty	Rebecca Winters
In the Boss's Castle	Jessica Gilmore
One Week with the French Tycoon	Christy McKellen
Rafael's Contract Bride	Nina Milne

HISTORICAL

In Bed with the Duke	Annie Burrows
More Than a Lover	Ann Lethbridge
Playing the Duke's Mistress	Eliza Redgold
The Blacksmith's Wife	Elisabeth Hobbes
That Despicable Rogue	Virginia Heath

MEDICAL

The Socialite's Secret	Carol Marinelli
London's Most Eligible Doctor	Annie O'Neil
Saving Maddie's Baby	Marion Lennox
A Sheikh to Capture Her Heart	Meredith Webber
Breaking All Their Rules	Sue MacKay
One Life-Changing Night	Louisa Heaton

MILLS & BOON®
Hardback – October 2016

ROMANCE

MILLS & BOON®
Large Print – October 2016

ROMANCE

Wallflower, Widow...Wife!	Ann Lethbridge
Bought for the Greek's Revenge	Lynne Graham
An Heir to Make a Marriage	Abby Green
The Greek's Nine-Month Redemption	Maisey Yates
Expecting a Royal Scandal	Caitlin Crews
Return of the Untamed Billionaire	Carol Marinelli
Signed Over to Santino	Maya Blake
Wedded, Bedded, Betrayed	Michelle Smart
The Greek's Nine-Month Surprise	Jennifer Faye
A Baby to Save Their Marriage	Scarlet Wilson
Stranded with Her Rescuer	Nikki Logan
Expecting the Fellani Heir	Lucy Gordon

HISTORICAL

The Many Sins of Cris de Feaux	Louise Allen
Scandal at the Midsummer Ball	Marguerite Kaye & Bronwyn Scott
Marriage Made in Hope	Sophia James
The Highland Laird's Bride	Nicole Locke
An Unsuitable Duchess	Laurie Benson

MEDICAL

Seduced by the Heart Surgeon	Carol Marinelli
Falling for the Single Dad	Emily Forbes
The Fling That Changed Everything	Alison Roberts
A Child to Open Their Hearts	Marion Lennox
The Greek Doctor's Secret Son	Jennifer Taylor
Caught in a Storm of Passion	Lucy Ryder

0916 GEN STD LP

MILLS & BOON®

Why shop at millsandboon.co.uk?

Each year, thousands of romance readers find their perfect read at millsandboon.co.uk. That's because we're passionate about bringing you the very best romantic fiction. Here are some of the advantages of shopping at www.millsandboon.co.uk:

* **Get new books first**—you'll be able to buy your favourite books one month before they hit the shops

* **Get exclusive discounts**—you'll also be able to buy our specially created monthly collections, with up to 50% off the RRP

* **Find your favourite authors**—latest news, interviews and new releases for all your favourite authors and series on our website, plus ideas for what to try next

* **Join in**—once you've bought your favourite books, don't forget to register with us to rate, review and join in the discussions

Visit **www.millsandboon.co.uk**
for all this and more today!